Nylon Rope

Sujatha (1935–2008) was the pseudonym of the Tamil author S. Rangarajan. He was one of the most popular authors in Tamil literature and his literary career spanned more than four decades. Widely-read and knowledgeable, his versatility and exhaustive range were his unique selling points.

Writing in simple and lucid Tamil, Sujatha made a tremendous impact with his contemporary and racy writing, and his radical and original ideas. His experiments with different genres, and the dramatic narration of ordinary, everyday events won him his audience and many accolades. His works stood out at a time when Tamil writing was dominated by social and family dramas and historical novels. His identification with the masses, and his depiction of their way of talking, behaviour, mindset, dialect and slang, helped make him popular across multiple demographic segments.

Suganthy Krishnamachari is a Chennai-based journalist, and has written articles on history, temple architecture, Sanskrit, mathematics, literature and music. She has written a series of books for schoolchildren on mathematics and English grammar. One of her short stories, published in a leading newspaper, is being used by an educational publishing company which is bringing out two English Language Teaching (ELT) series for school students. Another story was translated into Tamil some years ago, and published by an educationist in a magazine he edits.

Nylon Rope

Sujatha

Translated by
Suganthy Krishnamachari

Published by
Rupa Publications India Pvt. Ltd 2023
7/16, Ansari Road, Daryaganj
New Delhi 110002

Sales centres:
Bengaluru Chennai
Hyderabad Jaipur Kathmandu
Kolkata Mumbai Prayagraj

Copyright © Sujatha 2017

This is a work of fiction. Names, characters, places and incidents are either the
product of the author's imagination or are used fictitiously and any resemblance
to any actual person, living or dead, events or locales is entirely coincidental.

All rights reserved.
No part of this publication may be reproduced, transmitted or stored in a retrieval
system, in any form or by any means, electronic, mechanical, photocopying,
recording or otherwise, without the prior permission of the publisher.

P-ISBN: 978-93-5702-793-9
E-ISBN: 978-93-5702-714-4

First impression 2023

10 9 8 7 6 5 4 3 2 1

First published Nylon Kayiru in the magazine Kumudham, 1968
First published in English by Westland Publications Ltd
in association with Mysticswrite 2017
Published in English by Rupa Publications India Pvt. Ltd
in association with Mysticswrite Pvt Ltd 2023

The moral right of the author has been asserted.

Printed in India
This book is sold subject to the condition that it shall not,
by way of trade or otherwise, be lent, resold, hired out or otherwise
circulated, without the publisher's prior consent, in any form of binding
or cover other than that in which it is published.

Contents

1. Walk, Don't Run — 2
2. Where Were You? — 9
3. Jawaharlal Nehru — 16
4. Embedded in the Wall — 25
5. 302 — 34
6. Letters — 42
7. Judgement at 8.45 — 51
8. Incarnation of Yama — 60
9. Ramanathan — 68
10. Motive for the Murder — 79
11. Needed, Click — 88
12. You've Come to the Wrong Place, Mister — 95
13. Sunanda's Diary — 103
14. Edifice of Cards — 110

From Sunanda's diary

18.09.1965

I'm eighteen years old. How I've changed over the years! I can no longer wear the blouses I wore last year. I've grown taller too. I feel shy when I see myself in the mirror, whether with my clothes on or in a state of undress. And yet, I want to continue to look at myself in the mirror. I am no longer interested in listening to songs on Radio Ceylon. I sit on the veranda, staring at men, and rating them. I tend to compare them with 'him'. In the last one week, I have felt as if fresh blood has begun to course through my veins. For some reason, I've been dressing up in different ways.

My dear Sunanda. You're mad. Mad about what? No, don't put that down. Do not use that word!

I've begun to read the book he gave me. Secretly, of course!

1

Walk, Don't Run

Place: Bombay
Time: 7.36 p.m.

He walked some distance. He stopped a taxi. Flipped the meter himself, got in, and closed the door.

'Pedder Road.'

The taxi took a U turn, came to second, then third gear, picked up speed, waited when the signal showed red, slipped through when the red turned to amber, and when the light turned green, the car sped away, mimicking jazz music in its speed.

You will not be able to guess what he was about to do. What was he about to do? The moment the car crossed the flyover and entered Pedder Road, he asked the driver to slow down. He looked at the high-rise buildings—fifteen floors, ten floors, nine. He asked the driver to stop in front of a building. He got down. He gave the driver five rupees. Refused to take the change. He walked.

A slow, steady, determined walk, which showed his

commitment to the task he had set himself, his belief in the need for it, his pride in what he was about to do.

He stood before a building that bore the name 'Tivoli Gardens'. Outside the building were the nameplates and he scanned them for a name. He found it—fifth floor, third block.

He pressed number five in the lift. The door closed, obscuring him from view, and took off. As the doors of the lift opened on the fifth floor, he noticed someone approaching. Immediately he pressed number six. The door closed. He got off on the sixth floor. No one saw him come out of the lift. He looked at his watch. He paused for twenty-five seconds. Using the staircase, he descended to the fifth floor.

There was no one on the fifth floor now. He walked slowly, the cool, fluorescent light providing the necessary illumination. In the distance was the sea. Its dashing waves could be heard faintly. There was no other noise. All the doors looked similar, and he looked at the brass plates which had the apartment numbers on them ... 500 ... he felt ... 501 ... a sense of nervous ... 502 ... excitement gripping him ... 503!

A door with a Formica veneer. A nameplate with the name G. N. Krishnan on it. He pressed the doorbell with his thumb. The bell's musical chime could be heard inside the apartment. He wiped his hands. Pressed again.

Ding dong.

The door opened. The one who opened the door is not our hero. In fact, start counting up to five hundred. Before you are done, he will be dead.

He must be thirty years old. Thin. Attractive face. An

endearing baldness. A shirt with a floral pattern. Cigarette dangling from his lips. 'Yes?' he said, the blue smoke playing around his lips.

But he identified the visitor at once.

'Oh my God! Good old J! What a pleasant surprise! Come in. Come in.'

The visitor laughed. 'Long time since we met.'

'Years. Years. Do sit down. What'll you have? Coffee? Or something more exciting?'

'I haven't come to have coffee, Krishnan. I want to ask you—'

'Make yourself comfortable first. Just a minute.' A kettle whistled. Krishnan went in. The visitor looked round the room. There was a purpose to his glance. It was clearly a rich man's room. Linoleum on the floor. A brick red carpet. The wall was painted with distemper, in a pleasing shade of blue. There was just one picture on the wall—a copy of a Cezanne painting. A huge radiogram. Fridge. The door to the room on the left was open. The bed there was broader than necessary for one person. On the varnished table—an American newspaper. Curtains. Dim lights.

Krishnan came back. 'What'll you have? Whisky?'

'I don't drink.'

'I have a liquor permit. Legally-sanctioned intoxication! Ha! Ha!' he laughed.

'Krishnan. Is that a radiogram?'

'Yes. I have lots of records. All of them are Western music. Do you like instrumental?'

'I do.'

'Shall I play something?'

'Okay.'

He opened the door of the record player. He pulled out many records with attractive jackets, and placed them before the visitor. 'Choose. Are you sure you don't want whisky? Difficult to get in Bombay. Scotch,' he said.

'No. I don't want whisky.'

'Okay. Let me mix a drink for myself. I'm making coffee for you in the percolator. It'll be ready soon.'

He pulled out a bottle of whisky from the fridge, poured some into a glass, topped it with soda, and sat down on the sofa.

'Well, J! You're silent.'

'Krishnan, are you expecting someone?'

'Not for another hour.'

'Is the door closed?'

'Yes. I say ... what is this? Some kind of James Bond task?'

'No,' he said, looking at the records, without touching any of them.

'We're meeting after so long. How's your sister?' asked Krishnan.

He didn't answer this question. 'Why don't you play this record?' he said. It was the one on top of the pile of records.

Walk, Don't Run—it was an album by the instrumental band The Ventures. Six songs on each side of the record.

'You like Ventures? Good!'

Krishnan opened the record player, put the record on it,

and clicked the 'automatic' button. The machine began doing its work. The cartridge moved aside. The bakelite tone arm moved and the stylus made a soft landing on the edge of the record, and glided along the inward spiraling grooves, picking up the vibrations, and converting them to music. The sound of guitars burst forth. Double bass and jazz drums joined in. Krishnan came back to the sofa and sat down.

The visitor: 'Turn up the volume.'

'More?'

'Yes. I like loud music.'

Krishnan turned the volume up. The guitar strings thundered. Slowly the visitor edged close to Krishnan. As Krishnan fiddled with the knobs, the visitor pulled out a nylon rope from his pocket. It was two-and-a-half feet in length, with the thickness of a thumb. In half a second, he looped the rope around Krishnan's neck, and tightened it.

What lovely music! The gasping sounds Krishnan made were drowned in the music.

Lovely music. The rope tightened further.

Rab-dee-rab-dee-ram, boomed the jazz drums. Krishnan tried to grip the strong arms behind him.

Guitar! Guitar! Guitar! Four youngsters who had got together to play the guitar! A flood of music. Krishnan could not withstand that tightness even for three minutes. *Karaboom*. He fell down. Lifeless.

The visitor wiped the sweat on his forehead. He loosened the rope. Looked at his watch. Went to the door. Dropped the rope into his pocket. He opened the door, and looked round.

There was no one. He closed the door. Walked swiftly to the lift. He pressed the button. One … two … three … the lights highlighted the numbers. The lift reached the fifth floor; he got in, and the door closed.

He got out of the lift, melted into the teeming crowds of Bombay.

In the apartment, the record player was now playing the second song.

The coffee in the percolator was bubbling.

From Sunanda's diary

They are all in the next room, playing bridge. I'm in this room, reading a book. I can see him in the mirror in the living room. He's smiling at me. He's smiled at me many times, but this time there is something different about his smile. I don't quite know what to make of it. But I like it.

He, my brother and I go to films together. When he and I are not alone, he is a different person altogether. When we are not alone, he doesn't sit beside me. He talks only with my brother. But when he and I are alone, he is like a tiger. A tiger hiding in the shadows, biding its time.

One thing is clear—he loves me. But does he love me, or is it just my body he loves? 'Love'—to me it remains one of those words one comes across in books. There was no 'love' in the smile he just gave me. What am I going to do?

2

Where Were You?

Harini (age twenty-eight, looks more like twenty-four). She got into the bus at Sion. It was a double-decker bus, and she went up to the top deck. She drew many stares. Lusty stares.

The reasons: her dress, the smell of the eau de cologne which she had daubed on her skin, her shampooed, wavy hair bouncing in the wind.

Harini was used to such stares. She didn't look at anyone. She adjusted her clothing. She pulled out a Perry Mason novel from her handbag, got to the bookmarked page, and began to read. It would take at least half an hour for the bus to reach Pedder Road. She could read fifteen to twenty pages in that time. It would keep her from thinking about Krishnan, whom she was going to meet.

Mason: I object. The question is not relevant to this case.

Look at her pretty face. You would definitely have seen her, especially if you are a cinema buff. She is the model in all those ad films one sees before the start of a film. She is a model with J. J. Publicity.

In a way, hers was a tragic life. Born in Goa, she had come

to Bombay, had met the wrong people, had learnt artifice, and, at the age of twenty-eight (a man seated himself beside her, although there were many other vacant seats in the bus), had been exposed to the seamier side of life, had slept during the day and kept awake at night, had found herself a job, and had put a considerable distance between herself and the idealized Indian womanhood, as seen in the likes of Savitri and Kannagi.

She first met Krishnan when her brother began to learn how to play the guitar from him. The first meeting began with a 'Hello', and later went beyond just friendship. She had even thought of marrying Krishnan. Once, Krishnan, when drunk, had even whispered a proposal to her. But it was all over now. Krishnan was going to marry a Malayali girl called Bhamini next month.

Harini couldn't concentrate on the Perry Mason book. *You're thinking of getting married, are you, you bastard? Don't think you can cast me aside like old clothes. You know nothing about my anger. I'm a bad enemy to have. I have your letters. Your pictures. I am going to use them. My dear Krishnan, I cost money* … she rehearsed what she was going to say to Krishnan.

Her last meeting with him came to mind. *Don't think about him. Read the book.*

Mason: Where were you on the night of the 15th?

Harini blushed as she recalled where she had been on the night of the 15th.

As the lift made its way up to the fifth floor, Harini's anger increased in intensity. She walked briskly.

Number 503. She pressed the doorbell.

Ding-dong.

She waited.

She pressed the bell again. No response. She knocked on the door. It opened. Was there no one in the room? 'Krishnan,' she called out hesitantly.

Chruk-chruk—the sound of the record player when the end of a record has been reached.

Krishnan.

That's when she noticed him on the floor. Why was he lying on the floor? Was he drunk? She sat down, turned him over.

Familiar face.

Open mouth.

Staring eyes.

Staring eyes.

Staring eyes.

It took some time for her to realize what had happened. She had never seen a corpse at such close quarters. When she realized he was dead, she said, 'Oh my God! I didn't do it. I didn't do it. I didn't do it. Where's my handbag? What am I going to do? What should one do in such circumstances? No. Don't look at the body. Should I scream? I don't know what I should do. Where's my handkerchief?'

She pulled out her handkerchief from where it had been nestling—between her breasts. It was drenched with sweat. She felt panicky. What did she need now? A telephone. Yes. A telephone. Whom should she call? Not the police. She decided to call Dev and do as he advised.

She looked at the entrance to the flat. The door had closed. There was a telephone in the room. Beside it was the telephone directory. The telephone number of the police helpline was on the first page. She skipped it, and began to look for the phone number of Trincas Restaurant.

Trim parlour.

Trim traders.

Trincas—532816.

Her hands shook as she dialled the number. The call went through.

Roses are red, my love.
Blue bells are blue.
Sugar is sweet, my dear, but
Nothing's as sweet as you.

~

Sax, piano, guitar, drums—Dev was singing to the accompaniment of the instruments. He marked the beat of each song by snapping his fingers.

Trincas. T R I NC A S. Only a few in the restaurant were listening to the music. Some were engaged in conversations. Men, women. Men staring at the red, painted lips of the women. Women who could read desire behind those stares. Trincas was the favourite haunt of the uppermost crust of Bombay's rich. An obscenely expensive restaurant. After midnight, there would be a cabaret there.

Dev. Done with the vocals, he sat at the piano. That's when the phone rang. Because of the noise in the restaurant, it took a few seconds for the young man at the billing counter to hear the phone ring.

'Trincas. Good evening.'

'.........'

'Who?'

'.........'

'Dev? Oh yes, just wait a minute.'

He scribbled a message on a slip of paper, and sent it to Dev. Dev had a look at the paper, but did not stop playing. He signalled to the young man that he'd had a look at the message.

The young man went back to the telephone. 'Miss. He's in the middle of a song. Please wait. He'll take the call when the song ends. Here he is.'

'Who is it?' asked Dev.

'A woman. Pleasant voice. She is in a mighty hurry.'

'Hello?'

'......'

'Oh, Harini. What's the matter?'

'...............'

'Harini! Is this true? Where are you now? Just a minute. Let me talk to you from another phone. Put down the phone and call 532817. Don't worry. Don't get agitated.'

He put down the receiver, ran past the pantry, took the wooden staircase three steps at a time, and entered the office room. There was no one there. Just as he entered, the phone rang, and he picked it up.

'Now tell me what happened, Harini.'

'Are you sure he's dead?'

'...'

'Okay. Listen to me carefully, Harini. You should never have gone there. I thought it was all over between the two of you. Did you touch anything there?'

'...'

'Stupid girl. What else did you touch? All right. You idiot. Listen to me. Don't touch anything else there. Don't touch anything. Pick up your handbag.'

'...'

'Look here. You mustn't cry. Afraid? Of what? I'll take care of everything. In two seconds, get the hell out of there. You should never have gone there. Leave the place. Don't use the lift. Use the staircase. Take a taxi. Come home. I'll leave the restaurant right away. Harini, you've done nothing. I know. Don't waste time. Hurry up. Leave the place.'

He put down the receiver. He craved a cigarette. 'Stupid bum,' he exclaimed, put a cigarette in his mouth, lit it, and thought for a few seconds. He looked at his watch.

He tried to recall where he'd been for the last one-and-a-half hours.

From Sunanda's diary

Dear Sir! You are reading my diary without my permission. It is wrong. It is a sin. Stop. Otherwise you will hang upside down in hell for a thousand years.

Saw Jai after a long time. I had just bought the latest *Eve's Weekly* from Novelty Book Shop and had stepped out, when I saw Jai in the distance. I crossed the road, pretended I hadn't seen him, and walked away. I know it was very wrong of me. How surprised Jai was! I had had a lengthy conversation with him the previous month. What is the use? What is the use of just talking with someone?

……… is a man of action.

Postscript: Vatsala is an idiot.

3

Jawaharlal Nehru

Inspector Madhavan (Bombay Police Crime Branch, Gamdevi division) arrived. There were nine or ten people outside the building. One of them was smoking, but when he saw the police jeep, he dropped his cigarette, stubbed it out, and walked up to the jeep. The policemen jumped out of the jeep. A few adjusted their belts.

'Where?' asked Madhavan.

'Fifth floor, third flat.'

'Is this the only entrance to the building?'

'No. There is a rear entrance and an iron staircase.'

'Show it to this constable.' He summoned a constable.

'Two of you remain here. Don't let anyone leave the building,' he said to two other constables.

Why am I taking all these precautions? Was the murderer a fool? He would have left long ago. Was it a man or a woman?

The wagon of the flying squad screeched to a halt. Two men got out and saluted Madhavan. *Lazy fellows. They have taken so long to come,* thought Madhavan. As if reading his thoughts, one of the men said, 'There was a riot near Opera House.

We were on our way there, when we received your radio message.'

'Let's go.'

Madhavan was silent as the lift went up. Another corpse. How many had he seen in his career? He couldn't recall.

When he came out of the lift on the fifth floor, he asked, 'Who called the police?'

One of the five men there came forward hesitantly and said, 'I did.'

'Who are you?'

'My name's Sheroor. I'm the manager of this building. When Das told me—'

'Who's Das?'

'I am Das,' another man stepped forward.

'Your full name?'

'Mangal Das.'

To the constable, Madhavan said: 'Don't write down anything now. He is hesitating.'

'I work in Hotel Rani, across the road. On days when Mr. Krishnan didn't go out for dinner, he would order from our hotel. I wanted to check if he wanted me to bring him dinner tonight. I pressed the doorbell. No response. I checked to see if the door was locked. The door opened. Inside ... inside ...'

'Did you touch anything in the room?'

'No sir. I ran to Mr. Sheroor and told him what I'd seen.'

'Okay. I'll have to ask you all some questions later. So stay here. This is the flat?'

'Yes.'

Madhavan told the constables to stay outside the flat. He went in.

He looked at the body. He looked around the room. He looked at the body again. He looked at the neck. The red weal on the neck. The record player was still running. The man was lying on his back. A glass of whisky on the table ... Eyes were open. *Must check if he had a liquor permit.* One of the man's slippers had come off his foot and was lying beside him. A bathroom on the opposite side. One leg was bent at the knee. A cigarette butt (filter)—burnt out—lay beside him. His cupped hand resembled a lotus with its petals open. *Ah, those eyes!*

Must arrange to have fingerprints lifted. Mustn't touch anything. Hello! What's this? Shoeprints on the linoleum, a few feet away from the tea table. He skirted round them, came out, and asked a constable for a piece of chalk. For a tape. He took off his shoes and went back into the flat with just his socks on. He drew a circle around the shoeprints he had seen. He searched for more shoeprints. He marked out his own shoeprints with a series of 'x's. Came out. 'Is there a phone in the neighbouring flat?'

'You can use the phone here, sir.'

'I don't want to use this phone.'

'All right. Come with me,' said Sheroor. Madhavan dialled a number and said, 'May I speak to Nambiar?'

'Speaking.'

'Good evening, sir. This is Inspector Madhavan, Gamdevi Crime Branch. Calling from a flat in Pedder Road.'

'Yes?'

'There is a dead man here. I think it is a case of strangulation. We must have an inquest.'

'Now?'

'Yes, now. I'll have to send the body for a post-mortem ... Lots of work.'

'All right. Send for an ambulance. Find three or four reliable witnesses. I'll be there in fifteen minutes. Okay?'

'Okay, sir.'

'Which place is this?'

'Number 503, Tivoli Gardens, Pedder Road.'

'All right. I'll be there.'

Madhavan phoned for an ambulance, and then came back to flat number 503.

Should he wait ... or start questioning the people there? He needed some dependable people for the inquest. He could include four men from this building ...

Madhavan looked out through the open window. In the distance, he saw a neon light blinking.

Another murder. Another murder. Where is the murderer? In Bombay? What's he doing now? Is he lighting a cigarette? Is he smiling? Where is that X? Is he sleeping soundly under a mosquito net? Or is he having nightmares? He? She?

He'll have to find that one man in the teeming population of Bombay. He would have to find him and say, 'You did it. You did it.' He'd have to arrest him, take him to court, get him sentenced to death by hanging. Or get him a sentence of imprisonment for 45,000 days. And then he and his department would have a sense of satisfaction.

Madhavan came out of the room.

The people outside stopped their conversation abruptly.

'Did any of you see any stranger enter or leave the building?'

They looked at each other. *Sheep*, Madhavan said to himself. One of them said, 'I saw a young woman.'

'Her name?'

'I don't know.'

'Your name?'

'Madhusudanan.'

'When did you see her?'

'Around 8.30. She ran down the stairs.'

'Age? Describe her.'

'Young woman. Very pretty. Bobbed hair …'

'Where were you at the time?'

'I was on the ground floor, waiting for the lift.'

'Mr. Sheroor. Does this lift not have an attendant?'

'He's on duty till six-thirty in the evening. After that it's self service.'

'Did no one else live with Krishnan?'

'No, sir. He was a bachelor.'

'Relatives?'

'No one lived in his flat with him. He had lots of friends.'

'Here we are,' said coroner Nambiar, making his entry. 'We've met before,' he said to Madhavan.

'Yes. That case of suicide.'

'And now, it's a murder, is it?'

'I think so,' said Madhavan, taking Nambiar into the flat and pointing to the corpse.

Nambiar gave a whistle, and said, 'He looks beautiful. Have you arranged to dust the place with fingerprint powder?'

'Going to do it now.'

Nambiar kneeled before the dead man. He pulled up the man's eyelids, shone a torch into his eyes. No corneal reflex. Felt his pulse. Put his ear to the man's chest.

'He's dead,' he pronounced.

'There can't be a truer statement.'

'Have you sent for an ambulance?'

'Yes.'

'Have you assembled some men? Shall we start the inquest?'

'Here,' said Madhavan, pointing to the group of men outside the flat.

'Just a minute. These chalk outlines?'

'The shoeprints are very clear,' said Madhavan.

Nambiar studied the shoeprints carefully. 'Any more such shoeprints in the room?'

'I didn't notice any other shoeprints.'

'We might see some more, once we dust the place with fingerprint powder. Hmm. Larger than size nine. Huge feet. Must have walked on wet sand ... Your friend must be a tall man.'

'Shall we look round the room?'

'Yes.'

They looked at the books on the shelf. *The Sexual Behaviour of the American Male*. Novels by Harold Robbins. *Sex Maniac*. A *Teach Yourself Hindi* book. 'Could be new to the city,' said Madhavan. 'What is this? Is it a book in Kannada or Malayalam?'

Bed. A broad one. Neat pillow cover. Refrigerator. Radiogram. 'Rich man. Must check if his purse is in his pocket. Must have a look at his cheque book.'

Picture on the wall.

Table ... a photo album, perhaps?

They had the whole night to turn the room inside out. They went back to the bookshelf. Notebooks. Letter pad. A pen, pencil. Nambiar flipped through the pages of the notebooks.

Six handkerchiefs.

Five vests.

'Laundry list.'

'What's this photo?'

A young woman. Clearly one accustomed to smiling for the camera. At the bottom of the photograph were the words: 'To the one and only Krishnan. With lots of love, Harini.'

A pack of cards. They opened the case. Out dropped fifty-two pictures of French men and women in erotic poses. Nambiar and Madhavan smiled at each other.

'He's a first-timer,' said Nambiar.

'Who?'

'The murderer. Look at the room. Whisky on the table. Records. Nothing's been disturbed. What does all this show? This is not an accidental murder. It's a premeditated murder. Murder by a man who had a strong motive for it.'

'I haven't thought much about this murder yet.'

The phone rang.

Madhavan let the phone ring a few times, and then picked it up.

'Hello?'
'Krishnan there?'
'Who are you?'
'A friend. Who are you?'
'Police. What's your name?'
'Jawaharlal Nehru.'
Click. The call was disconnected.
'Hello. Hello. Hello,' Madhavan kept repeating into the receiver.

From Sunanda's diary

Friday. 'Date With You' programme on the radio. Beatles' 'A Hard Day's Night'. At the end of the song, instrumental music producing the effect of falling leaves. Mala—my friend in college—how is it she has ... Wheat, she says! No falsies, she claims. Not necessary, she says. And then the other things Mala said. How could she say such things without blushing? The joke she cracked in the Chemistry lab! Smutty!

4
Embedded in the Wall

'Jawaharlal Nehru,' said Ganesh (age twenty-eight), and put down the phone.

Harini and her brother Dev didn't relish his levity.

Ganesh winked at Harini and said, 'The police are there.'

'So?'

'They will search the room. What will they find? Your picture. Your letters to Krishnan. Your brother Dev's threatening letter. And then the police will come looking for you …'

There was a knock on the door. 'Let me see if that's the police,' said Ganesh, as he got up to open the door. He was very tall.

Harini moved her chair closer to Dev's. 'What are we to do?' she asked.

'Sit tight,' said Dev.

The door opened. The coffee that Ganesh ordered had arrived.

'What you both need is some intelligence. And also some coffee.' He mixed the decoction and milk and asked, 'Tell me, Harini. How long had you known Krishnan?'

'Two years.'

'What kind of relationship was yours?'

'We were very close.'

'How close? What was the distance between the two of you—a foot, an inch, or zero?'

'The third.'

'I like clients who are straightforward,' said Ganesh. (He was a lawyer). 'All right. You are speaking the truth, aren't you, when you say he was dead when you reached the flat?'

'That's the truth. The absolute truth.'

'Why did you not inform the police at once?'

'My first instinct was to run away.'

'Did you run away?'

'I thought I'd consult Dev and then run away.'

Ganesh laughed. 'And what did Dev say?'

'To leave the place immediately.'

'Stupid thing to have done. You should have called the police at once. You've seen the dead man, but have come away without informing the police. Even a dull-witted man is bound to suspect you.'

'But no one knows I went to Krishnan's flat.'

'So?'

'What I mean is—why would the police suspect me?'

'You underestimate the police. When the case goes to court—'

'Court?' exclaimed Dev.

'Mr. Devduttan. I hope you haven't come to meet me just to have a cup of coffee. I don't think this is a simple open-

and-shut case. An elder brother. His sister is friendly with a man who gets murdered. The brother and sister come running to a lawyer. What does it mean?'

'Ganesh. You are reading between the lines.' Dev lit a cigarette, pulled on it and continued. 'I haven't come to be frightened by you. What should we do in the circumstances? That's what we want you to tell us. Otherwise, I'll find some other—'

'Wait. Don't get agitated. Your agitation will land you in trouble. You are my friend. Will I not help you? But I need to get a clearer picture, if I'm to help you. Dev, look at me and tell me honestly—did you kill Krishnan?'

'No,' said Dev, without looking at Ganesh.

'Look at me when you answer.'

'Will the police come here?' asked Harini.

'Here? To my office? No. But they'll be there at your place tomorrow. That's for sure.'

'Why?'

'To eat some chocolate,' said Ganesh.

Neither Dev nor Harini laughed.

'I thought that was a good joke. There's a childish innocence about you. I think I can trust you.'

'Ganesh, does that mean you suspect us?'

'I don't know. Okay, Harini. Krishnan and you have been intimate, haven't you?'

'Yes.'

'Any idea where he might have kept your letters?'

'Give me a second. Let me think.'

'Your time's up.'

'I saw a painting in Krishnan's room. There's a cupboard behind the painting. A built-in cupboard—a cupboard embedded in the wall. He used to keep letters and money in that cupboard.'

'A cupboard behind a painting?'

'Yes.'

'A locked cupboard?'

'Yes.'

'Embedded in the wall?'

'......'

'And usually the painting hides it from view?'

'Yes.'

'Excellent. Some reason to cheer. Unusual place. It'll take awhile for the police to find it. What's the time now? Eleven o'clock. I think the inquest will be tomorrow. Anyway, I'll be there two hours from now.'

'Where?'

'Krishnan's flat.'

'Ganesh! What kind of stunt is this?'

'Don't worry. I'm no ordinary lawyer. I aim to give satisfaction to my clients. Especially if they are women. More so if they are beautiful women.' Ganesh winked at Harini.

'Why should you go there?' asked Dev.

'If I am able to get those compromising letters out of the cupboard before the police find them, then that's the end of the matter as far as you are concerned.'

'I don't understand.'

'Tomorrow morning, you will see what I mean. Do you have a key to Krishnan's flat?'

An embarrassed Harini said, 'Yes.'

'Do you have it here with you?'

'Yes,' said Harini, and gave the key to Ganesh.

'Ganesh, if you are going to do what I think you are planning to do, you are sure to be caught,' said Dev.

'Do you know who I am? Ganesh! I am as slippery as an eel. I won't be caught. And if I am, I'll fling some legalese at them. Dev, when did you last see Krishnan?'

'This evening.'

'Oh dear. Where? At what time?'

'Five o'clock in the evening. His flat.'

'Oh dear. What happened when you met him?'

'Nothing. I loathed him … Harini and he … you know the story. I asked him how he could dump Harini and marry someone else.'

'And?'

'He pulled out his cheque book. I was furious. I ripped his shirt, slapped him, and said, "I'll deal with you later".'

'Did you hit him hard?'

'No. Just a mild slap.'

Ganesh sighed.

'Why? What's wrong?'

'Your fingerprints. Your threatening letter. You went there. Your sister went there too. What a tangle! Okay. What did you do then? This is very important …'

'I took a bus to Trincas. I played the piano there. Harini called. I went home. And now we are here.'

'You were in the restaurant for the rest of the evening, till nine o'clock?'

'Just a minute. What are you trying to say? That I killed Krishnan?'

'That's the conclusion the police are going to come to. We have to be prepared for that.'

'If that is the conclusion the police come to, then they are fools. I didn't kill that man. That's as true as the fact that you are your mother's son.'

'I know I'm my mother's son only because others say so! We'll worry about your alibi later. Now Ganesh is off on a mission.'

'Where are you going?' asked Harini.

'Flat number 503, Tivoli Gardens. To get your letters from that cupboard.'

'There'll be no one there now.'

'Let's see.'

'How will you open the locked cupboard?'

'When I was in Law College, my hobby was picking locks. Some will yield even to a small twine. I have a bunch of keys—five in all. Almost all locks can be opened with one or the other of these five keys. I'm another Houdini. When I retire, I am going to write a book on how to pick locks.'

'Will there be any risk?'

'Risk is my other name. Moreover, think of all the men who died for the sake of women. Helen of Troy, etc. Don't be afraid. Go home. I'll meet you tomorrow.'

'Ganesh, you are great.'

'Later on, when I ask you to pay me my legal fees, I'll also charge you for all these risks. Let's see what you say then. Good night.'

Ganesh got off the bus a furlong before Tivoli Gardens. He walked in the shadow of the buildings. He walked stealthily like a cat. Must have been two in the morning. There was a jeep outside the building. There was a policeman sitting on a stool, reading something. Ganesh made his way through a narrow gap between buildings and reached the rear entrance of Tivoli Gardens. He made his way up through the utility stairs. The door was locked on the inside. Sixth floor, seventh, eighth, ninth—the doors to all floors were locked. He made his way to the terrace. There should be a door leading to the terrace. And the staircase beside the lift should end here. He looked for the staircase, found it, unlocked the door and descended.

Which floor was this? Ten. Then nine, eight, seven, six, five. He peeped round the corner. A long corridor, the third flat on the left. There was a constable seated outside, his back to Ganesh.

Ganesh waited.

After exactly twenty-five minutes, the constable got up. Stretched his arms. Yawned. Looked round, and began walking away. Ganesh waited until he had left the corridor.

One second, two seconds, three, four seconds. Fourth second, he was outside Krishnan's flat. Fifth second, he took out the key to the apartment. Sixth second, he put the key in the keyhole. Eighth second, he opened the door. Ninth second, retrieved the key. Tenth second, he shut the door.

It was quiet inside the room. The bathroom light was on. It threw some feeble rays of light into the room. He noticed the chalk marks. The room was a mess. He looked for the painting Harini had mentioned. There it was. He moved the picture. Behind it was a keyhole. Two of the five keys he had with him fit the keyhole, but didn't open the lock. He gently turned the keys both ways. No use.

I've lost touch. My nervousness is a spoiler. He pressed the key. *Click.*

It opened.

Not the lock. The door to the flat.

A switch was turned on.

Bright light flooded the room.

From Sunanda's diary

We went to the Ram Lila celebrations. A far as I was concerned, it was more like Krishna Lila. He took advantage of the jostling crowds to brush against me, to press himself against me. I pretended I didn't notice. Where am I headed?

5
302

It was Inspector Madhavan who had switched on the light in the room. Ganesh recovered his composure and stuck his hands into his trouser pockets, trying to strike a casual pose like a visitor to an exhibition.

Madhavan was taken aback by his nonchalance. But his police training came to the rescue. 'Don't move.'

'I've come to meet Krishnan.'

'Hello! A guest! Hey you!' he called out to the constable outside. 'Who are you? How did you get in?' he asked Ganesh.

'I'm Ganesh, Krishnan's friend. I came to see Krishnan. What's this? The room is in total disarray. And the police here? Krishnan ... where is he?'

'He's dead.'

'Oh my God!' said Ganesh, clutching his heart.

'You're a miserable actor,' said Madhavan.

'I don't understand.'

To the constable, Madhavan said, 'Where were you? How did this man get in?'

The constable looked at Ganesh. He uttered some abusive words about Ganesh's parentage, and moved closer to him.

'Wait,' Madhavan said to the constable.

To Ganesh, 'What did you say your name was?'

'Ganesh.'

'I'll give you a minute. How did you get here? Why did you come here?'

'Question number one: how did I get here? I used the staircase.'

'Didn't you see any of the policemen posted outside?'

'No, I didn't. I walked here in a sleepy daze. I have a key to my friend Krishnan's flat. I entered and just when I was fumbling to find the switch, you—'

'Wasn't there a constable outside this flat?'

'No.'

'I went to the bathroom,' the constable said sheepishly.

'Idiot!' said Madhavan.

'Question number two: why did I come here? Sometimes I would sleep over in Krishnan's flat after watching the last show of a film. *How to Steal a Million*. Excellent film. Peter O'Toole. Never mind all that. You said Krishnan is dead ...'

'Mister. I know you are pretending that you didn't already know about Krishnan's death. You didn't come here to sleep. I must subject you to some special police treatment and interrogation.'

'Why should you do that?'

'To get the truth from you.'

'I'm speaking the truth now.'

35

'Are you joking?'

'Inspector, have you read *Pickwick Papers*?'

'I'm going to arrest you.'

'Do you have an arrest warrant? In accordance with Section 75, Cr. P. C.? '

'Oh, so you know the law. Haven't you heard of Section 54? It's possible to arrest a person without a warrant.'

'For what offence?'

'Oh, any number of offences: breaking into houses, preventing the police from doing their duty.'

'Your words surprise me, Inspector. Look at it from my angle. I come here to see my friend. I have a key to his flat. I enter the flat without anyone stopping me. Is it my fault that the constable was not outside the flat when I arrived? Have I stolen anything?'

'Constable, check if this man has stolen anything.'

The constable approached Ganesh gleefully.

'Don't touch me. I have only one good Terylene shirt. I'll show you what I have …'

The constable ignored him and pulled out from his pockets a purse, a diary, a comb.

'Inspector, you are treating me very badly. You'll have to face legal consequences for your actions.'

'Shut up, you rat!' said Madhavan. He chanced to look at Ganesh's calling card. 'Oh, a lawyer, are you?'

'Yes. There is an inspector I know of who arrested a man without a proper warrant. I filed a habeas corpus petition on behalf of the man. The arrested man had a weak heart.

He was carried off by a gentle blow from the inspector. A compensation of one hundred thousand rupees was awarded to the man's next of kin. Three constables and an inspector were dismissed from service. One hundred thousand. One followed by five zeroes.'

'Are you trying to frighten me? You will come to your senses if you spend a night in jail.'

'I'm speaking the truth.'

'I've heard your voice somewhere. Wait a minute. Oh, yes. Aren't you the one who spoke on the telephone?'

'Telephone?'

'You asked who was speaking and when I said "Police", you gave a childish reply. "Jawaharlal Nehru", you said.'

'Jawaharlal Nehru?'

'Yes.'

'Our dead prime minister Jawaharlal Nehru? If this is a joke, I must confess, I don't get it.'

'It annoys me even to look at you.'

'The feeling is mutual.'

The inspector thought for a few seconds.

'Write down your name and address. Leave your driving licence behind. Come to the Gamdevi police station at ten o'clock tomorrow. I want you to answer some questions. Who is your client?'

'No one. I watched a film, last show, and—'

'Constable, throw him out.'

'No need to. I'm leaving. May I use the phone?'

'No, you may not.'

'Good night, Inspector. Good night, 1357,' Ganesh winked at the constable, collected his belongings, ran a comb through his hair, and left.

'Sir, you shouldn't have let him go.'

'I wanted him out of the way. When I entered, he was looking for something behind that painting. Take down that painting from the wall.'

The constable took down the painting. The inspector noticed a cupboard behind it, twelve inches long, six inches wide, with its door now open. There were two bundles of letters in the cupboard. Two insurance policy certificates, bonds of the Kerala State Electricity Board, a cheque book. Some hundred-rupee notes, a small photo album, and some old coins. Madhavan opened a bundle of letters and began to read them. Most were written either by a girl called Harini or a girl called Maragatham. Smutty letters. One letter drew his attention. It was an angry letter from a man called Dev.

Harini told me yesterday that you offered to give her two thousand five hundred rupees, and that you wanted to continue the relationship with her even after your marriage. I'm shocked by your audacity and your arrogance. She says when she refused to go along with your suggestion, you threatened to get her sacked from J. J. Publicity. If something like that happens, I will kill you.

Dev

Inspector Madhavan laughed. 'Mister Ganesh. I know who your client is. Constable, I think the first arrests in this case will be made by tomorrow evening.'

Inspector Madhavan was seated before Balan, manager of J. J. Publicity.

'Does Miss Harini work here?'

'We dismissed her last week.'

The inspector had expected this reply.

'Do you know Mr. G. N. Krishnan?'

'Yes, he is a very close friend. Has he done something wrong?'

'He's dead. Haven't you seen the paper?'

'Oh, hell! When did this happen? How?'

'What kind of man was Krishnan?'

'I don't understand. What do you mean by that question?'

'His qualities.'

'He had some weaknesses.'

'Example?'

'Women. Wine. Money. Oh my God! Oh my God! He's dead? I can't believe it.'

'I want some details about Harini. What was her designation in this company?'

'She was an ad model. We would take pictures of her for ads. Sometimes, short films too.'

'Was there anything going on between Harini and Krishnan?'

'Plenty.'

'Did you dismiss Harini because Krishnan wanted you to?'

'In a way, yes. Krishnan is related to the managing director of this company.'

'Do you have her address?'

'Yes.'

At four-thirty in the evening, the phone rang in Ganesh's house.

'Yes?'

'Ganesh. This is Dev.'

'Yes?'

'They're here.'

'Who?'

'Police.'

'Police? What for?'

'To arrest me. They have a warrant. You lied to me this morning.'

'Dev, Dev. Don't worry.'

'How comforting your words are!'

'Listen, Dev. Go with them. But don't say anything to them. Don't answer their questions. Don't even answer innocuous questions like "Have you had a cup of coffee". Be silent like a lama. I'll be there right away. Don't resist arrest.'

'Ganesh. I don't know what is going on. One thing's clear—you've muddled everything up.'

'Have a look at the warrant. What does it say?'

'It has the magistrate's signature. It authorizes the police officer to arrest me. It has an official seal.'

'No, no. That's not what I wanted you to check out. What is the crime for which you are being arrested?'

'There's lots written in the warrant. Something about a Section 302.'

'Section 302 means murder.'

From Sunanda's diary

He comes home often. Smiles at me. I smile back at him. I often think of Jai too. Thinking of Jai doesn't disturb my conscience. But K.... On one side, Joyce's *Ulysses*, existentialism, and a whole lot of other things I can't understand. On the other side physical attraction, touches, pleasing torments, desires—this is the side my heart chooses to be on.

What shall I compare this to? The traffic signal shows red. But when there's no policeman around, we sometimes ignore the signal, don't we? It's similar to that. I'm writing this before going to bed. I'll be back to normal tomorrow morning.

6

Letters

It was an old building of stone and brick. A large room in the building. A fan hanging from the thirty-foot high ceiling. Beneath the fan was seated Presidency Magistrate Purushottam Haridas. (Age fifty-five. Coarse hair. Spectacles with a black and gold frame. Two rings in one finger.) Seated a little away from him was the court clerk. Before him a Remington typewriter. On the wall a picture of a smiling Mahatma Gandhi. Preliminary hearing in the case of State of Maharashatra versus Devdutt, son of Jayadev.

Public Prosecutor Mansukhani was putting his papers in order.

Ganesh (defence lawyer) was trying to fold a piece of paper into sixteen squares. That's when the magistrate asked him, 'Have you received all the reports and documents? Final report from the police, FIR, statements of the prosecution witnesses?'

'Yes, Your Honour.'

'Are you satisfied?'

'Only some portions of the statements of taxi driver Charandas and manager Sheroor have been given to us,' said Ganesh.

The magistrate looked at Mansukhani.

'Your Honour, only those portions of their statements that are relevant to the case have been given to the defence,' said Mansukhani.

'But I think some things are necessary. For example, only some letters from Krishnan's cupboard have been filed in court. All the letters taken from the cupboard in Krishnan's flat must be filed in court. It's important for the defence,' said Ganesh.

'That should not be a problem. Mr. Ganesh, what's your argument?'

Ganesh: 'My argument is that there is no prima facie evidence against my client. My only witness is the accused Devdutt.'

'Prosecution?'

'We have six witnesses, Your Honour.'

'Okay. Start your arguments. Remember. This is a preliminary. So make it short.'

Mansukhani put on his spectacles. 'The accused in this case—J. Devdutt. Krishnan—resident of Pedder Road, Tivoli Gardens, flat number 503 was—'

Ganesh got up. 'If prosecution is going to be allowed to open their arguments with a speech, I too must be given a chance to make a speech.'

Magistrate to Mansukhani: 'Bring in your witnesses. I don't think we need a preamble.'

A disappointed Mansukhani said, 'I'll call Inspector Madhavan.'

Madhavan stood in the witness box, confidence writ

large on his face. Answered questions put to him clearly. He mentioned the telephone call received by the police. He spoke of his visit to the flat, of what he saw, of the inquest ...

'Reports of the inquest, post-mortem report, etc., have all been filed in court,' said Mansukhani.

'I have seen them,' said Ganesh.

'What did you find when you inspected Krishnan's room?' Mansukhani asked Madhavan.

'The room presented an orderly sight. No attempt had been made to steal anything. The record player was running. There were glasses of whisky on the table. I could see shoeprints on the floor. Size nine. Huge feet. There were many letters in the cupboard. Most of them were by a woman called Harini,' said Madhavan.

'Did you enquire who Harini was?'

'The sister of Devdutt.'

'All right. The rest of the letters?'

'One was by Devdutt.'

'What did you infer from the letters?'

'Krishnan and Harini were in an intimate relationship. But Krishnan decided to marry someone else. This made Harini and her brother Devdutt angry. Harini was employed as a model in an ad agency. Recently she lost her job. Krishnan was responsible for her dismissal. Devdutt had threatened to kill Krishnan if he got Harini dismissed from her job. This letter from Devdutt was the basis of my suspicion of him.'

'That letter has been filed, Your Honour. Shall I read it out to you?' asked Mansukhani.

'No need to,' said Purushottam.

'What did further investigation reveal, Inspector?' asked Mansukhani.

'On the night of the murder, Devdutt was seen entering Krishnan's flat. A violent argument ensued between them.'

Ganesh got up. 'Your Honour. You mustn't allow this. This is hearsay. Summon the witnesses. Let's hear it from them.'

'This is only a preliminary hearing. We have statements given by them. The defence has also been given copies of these. If we were to summon every one of the witnesses questioned by the inspector, it will just lead to unnecessary delays.'

'No. I must be given an opportunity to cross-examine them. I must know under what circumstances their statements were recorded. You should definitely not allow this hearsay evidence.'

'Mr. Ganesh is right. Send for the people whose statements the inspector recorded,' said the magistrate.

'We are going to send for them, Your Honour. Okay. Let me rephrase my question. Inspector, you interrogated many people. What's the conclusion you came to? I'm sure the defence can't object to this.'

'Go ahead,' said Ganesh.

'On the night of the murder, around seven-thirty, Devdutt arrived at the building in a taxi. He went to Krishnan's flat. They had an argument. Devdutt exited the room in a hurry. The time of death given in the post-mortem report coincides more or less with the time Devdutt came to the flat. We lifted Devdutt's fingerprints from the room. His shoeprints were also clearly visible. The pattern on the bottom of his shoes matched the shoeprints on the floor,' said the inspector.

'Your Honour. It's the responsibility of the prosecution to prove every statement of the inspector's with corroborative evidence from an examination of the witnesses. If they are unable to do that, all of the inspector's inferences should be dismissed forthwith,' said Ganesh.

'We'll prove everything, Mr. Ganesh,' said Mansukhani. 'Don't worry. Every statement of the inspector's will be corroborated by the witnesses when they are cross-examined. Thank you, Inspector.' To Ganesh: 'You may go ahead with the cross-examination.'

'Inspector, what's your height?'

'Five feet ten inches.'

'The size of your shoes?'

'Nine.'

'The shoeprints in Krishnan's room could have been yours.'

'Not possible.'

'Why do you say so?'

'The pattern on my shoes is different. I noticed it soon after I entered the room. I also marked out the shoeprints at once.'

'Did you not walk around inside the room?'

'I did. But I took off my shoes soon after. And I marked out with crosses whatever marks my shoes had made.'

'Strange.'

'Nothing strange about it. That's what any careful policeman would do.'

'And you are claiming that the shoeprints you found are Devdutt's?'

'I'm not claiming it. I made a comparison of his shoes and the shoeprints in Krishnan's room, and they matched.'

'How can you say the shoeprints were left on the day of the murder? It's quite possible that Devdutt might have visited Krishnan the previous day and the shoeprints might have been left then.'

'Possible. But the room is cleaned every day.'

'Really? Did you find out at what time the room was cleaned on the day of the murder?'

'No.'

'Okay. These fingerprints. You said you found Devdutt's fingerprints in some places in the room. Who lifted the fingerprints? Forensic department?'

'No. We lifted the fingerprints ourselves. We sent them to the Forensic Department for confirmation that they were Devdutt's.'

'How were the fingerprints lifted?'

'Why? The usual way—using mercury chalk powder.'

'That's not what I meant. In whose presence were the fingerprints lifted?'

'In my presence by another police officer.'

'Were they taken in Krishnan's flat?'

'Yes. Later we took Devdutt's fingerprints and sent both to the Forensic Department for a comparison.'

'These fingerprints too—as in the case of the shoeprints—you can't say when they were left by my client, can you?'

'No.'

'You said when you entered Krishnan's flat, a record player was on. Was there a record on it?'

'Yes. An LP record.'

'Was it playing?'

'No. It had come to an end.'

'So it's quite possible that, during the murder, the record might have been playing?'

'Yes.'

'You mentioned many letters. Harini's. Devdutt's threatening letter. Were there any other letters?'

'Yes. There were other letters too.'

'Written by other women?'

'Yes.'

'Who are those women? Their names?'

'Can't remember all the names. Maragatham …'

'Inspector, how surprising! Should you not have questioned every one of those women? Isn't it possible that, like Harini and Devdutt, they too might have had a motive for murder?'

'That will depend on the relationship Krishnan had with those women.'

'Were the other letters love letters?'

'You could say so.'

'So the letters show that Krishnan was close to many women besides Harini and Maragatham, right?'

'In a sense.'

'They too might have resented Krishnan's forthcoming marriage, just as much as Devdutt did, right?'

'He's repeating the same question,' objected Mansukhani.

'Your Honour, you must dismiss this case at once. The police enquiry has not been impartial. It's been shoddy. It's not right to pick out only Harini and Devdutt and accuse them. Who are the other women? Where do they live? Where were they on the night of the murder? We know nothing about any of this. Until we gather all these details, they too should be in the category of suspects,' said Ganesh.

Mansukhani jumped up. 'The letters are not the only reason to suspect Devdutt. The post-mortem report gives the time of death. There are witnesses who saw Devdutt enter Krishnan's flat. There are people who heard them argue. All these people are going to be examined.'

'That's not my argument. An autopsy can give only an approximate time. Who were the people who came to Krishnan's flat? What was the connection between Krishnan and those people? Did those people have pretty sisters too? Did they have reason to dislike Krishnan? Should we not consider all these factors too?'

From Sunanda's diary

Why am I writing this diary? This is not the way to write a diary. I'm writing this diary while thinking of those who are going to read it in the future. This is not right. I should record my thoughts honestly, shouldn't I?

7
Judgement at 8.45

'Your point is well taken,' said the magistrate to Ganesh. 'But the aim of this preliminary hearing is to examine whether there is enough evidence to commit the case to the Sessions Court. So we have to take into consideration all evidence which the prosecution brings forward. We can't question why they haven't brought in more evidence. Proceed.'

'Have you completed the cross-examination of the inspector?' Mansukhani asked Ganesh.

'I want to question the inspector again after other witnesses have been examined,' said Ganesh.

The next witness was taxi driver Charandas. He said, in reply to the public prosecutor's questions, that he had picked up a tall man on Mahatma Gandhi Road at seven-thirty on the night of the murder. He identified Devdutt as the man he had picked up.

Ganesh began his cross-examination of Charandas.

'Charandas, where were you at seven-thirty in the evening yesterday?'

'In my taxi.'

'Yes, in your taxi, but where were you? That's my question.'

'Girgaum, I think.'

'You think?'

'Yes. Since I am always on the move, it's hard to say exactly where I was.'

'Then how is it that you remember where you were on the night of the murder?'

'I don't understand your question.'

'Is there any particular reason why you remember that it was Devdutt you picked up on the night of the murder?'

'I read about the murder in the papers the next day. I recalled that I had dropped off a man at the building where the murder had taken place. I wondered if there might be some connection between the murder and my passenger. So I went to the nearest police station and told them about the man I'd dropped off at the building.'

'I see. When did you first see Devdutt?'

'At the police station.'

'Gamdevi police station?'

'Yes.'

Mansukhani was fretting.

'You'd not seen him before?'

'No. I hadn't. No, no. I saw him when I picked him up. That was when I first saw him. I forgot completely.'

'Forgot?'

'Yes. I forgot. I first saw him when he got into my taxi. Then I saw him again at the police station.'

'You saw him on Mahatma Gandhi Road at seven-thirty in the evening, right?'

'Yes.'

'Where on Mahtama Gandhi Road did he get into your taxi?'

'Near Jehangir Art Gallery. Near the IAC office.'

'Was that part of the road well lit?'

'It usually is.'

'You saw him at seven-thirty in the evening. He got into your taxi. You remember his face clearly.'

'Yes,' said Charandas, looking at Devdutt.

'Was there enough light for you to see him clearly?'

'Yes.'

'So you remember the face of a man who boarded your taxi at seven-thirty on a certain night last month?'

'Yes.'

'All right. Describe the person who got into your taxi at ten in the morning yesterday.'

Mansukhani interrupted: 'Your Honour, this is a sheer waste of time. He remembers Devdutt. My friend is repeating the same question.'

Unmindful of the interruption from Mansukhani, Ganesh continued with his questioning of Charandas.

'When you saw Devdutt at the police station, what did they ask you?'

'Who?'

'The police. Did they say, "Is this the man who got into your taxi?"'

'Yes, that's what they asked me.'

'And you said that this was the man who had been your passenger the previous night.'

'Yes, that's right.'

'Was Devdutt pointed out to you when they put the question to you? Or were there other men there, and did the police perhaps ask you which of them had been your passenger the previous night?'

'No. There were no others. Devdutt was the only one there at the police station.'

'I can say with confidence that you saw Devdutt for the first time at the police station. Didn't the police say, "Give a statement that this man here is the one you picked up yesterday night and we will withdraw the case filed against you for drunken driving"?'

'This is too much, Your Honour,' protested Mansukhani.

'Mr. Ganesh. Do not ask irrelevant questions,' said the magistrate.

'Sorry. This man is a liar. Look at his records. He is a consistent liar.'

'Leave such conclusions to me,' said the magistrate.

'I have just one more question, Charandas. What is the registration number of your taxi?'

'MRT 1387.'

'1387 or 1378?'

'1378.'

'But you just said 1387.'

'78 ... 8 ...'

'Your Honour, this man has very poor memory power. That's all, Your Honour.'

R. A. Sheroor came in next. He confirmed that he was

the manager of Tivoli Gardens, and that on the night of the murder, he had seen Devdutt enter Krishnan's flat at seven-thirty in the evening.

'Where's Krishnan's flat?' Ganesh began his cross-examination of Sheroor.

'Fifth floor.'

'What were you doing on the fifth floor at seven-thirty in the evening?'

'I was told there was a problem with a tap in the second flat.'

'Who told you that? The police?'

'No.'

'Do you know plumbing?'

'No.'

'How do you know you were there at seven-thirty? It could have been five-thirty.'

'I noted the time.'

'Why?'

'Because I wanted to know the time.'

'Mr. Sheroor. You went to the fifth floor to fix a tap. You saw Devdutt enter Krishnan's flat. You immediately noted the time. Sounds contrived, doesn't it?'

'That's what happened.'

'What's the time now? Look at your watch and tell me.'

Sheroor was not wearing a watch.

'You said you noted the time. Did you consult your watch or the wall clock in the corridor?'

'The wall clock.'

'There is no wall clock in the corridor. Thank you, Mr. Sheroor.'

Sheroor's evidence lay in tatters.

Ganesh examined the other witnesses breezily. The Parsi lady, Mrs. Dastur, who lived in the flat next to Krishnan's and who claimed to have heard an argument in Krishnan's flat, was the next witness.

Here are some of the questions Ganesh asked her:

'Mrs. Dastur. When did you hear the argument in Krishnan's flat?'

'The night Krishnan died.'

'What day of the week was it?'

'Wednesday.'

'Wednesday?'

'Yes, I think it was Wednesday.'

'Since you are recalling something that took place a month ago, maybe your memory is playing tricks on you?'

'No, no. It was a Wednesday.'

'You live in flat number 501.'

'No, no. 502.'

'Sorry, 502. Can you hear what happens in the flat next to yours?'

'To some extent.'

'Was the voice you heard one you were familiar with?'

'No.'

'So how do you know it was an argument between Devdutt and Krishnan?'

'I never said it was. I heard an argument. I then saw Devdutt leave Krishnan's flat angrily.'

'Never mind. During the argument, did you hear anything else?'

'No.'

'Are you certain? Radio? Record player?'

'No.'

'Didn't you hear any music?'

'No. I only heard them argue.'

'Thank you, Mrs. Dastur.'

Manuskhani said, 'Your Honour. The prosecution submission is over.'

'Your witness,' said the magistrate to Ganesh.

'I have only one witness, and that is the accused Devdutt,' said Ganesh.

'You don't have to go into the witness box. You have certain rights. You can refuse to give evidence. You know that, don't you?' said the magistrate to Devdutt.

'I know, Your Honour.'

'Okay. Proceed.'

Devdutt said he had been to Krishnan's flat on the evening of the murder. He was there at five o'clock, he said.

'What happened when you went there?'

'I asked Krishnan how he could treat my sister so badly. I spoke to him angrily.'

'Was there an argument between the two of you?'

'Yes, there was.'

'And?'

'He tore out a leaf from his cheque book. I shouted at him and left.'

'What time was it then?'

'Five-thirty.'

'What did you do when you left Krishnan's flat?'

'I took a bus to Trincas Restaurant.'

'What did you do there?'

'I played the piano.'

'Until what time?'

'Till nine o'clock.'

'Is it possible for you to leave the restaurant?'

'It's not possible because I have signed a contract with Trincas. According to the terms of that contract, I have got to be there at a certain time, and I've got to play and sing for a certain number of hours. Every day.'

'Mr. Devdutt. Did you murder Krishnan?'

'No. I didn't. I want to live. I'm in love with life. I have many desires in life. I respect human life.'

'You can cross-examine him,' said Ganesh to Mansukhani.

From Sunanda's diary

My brother is going to Chandigarh. For three days. I'm going to be alone for three days. Three days! I begged him to take me along with him. He refused. It's an official tour, he said. How will I make him understand? The state I am in ... My inability to resist ... In case ...

What am I afraid of? That I will lose my self-control? Have I no faith in myself? Jai—I must see you. If I do, everything will be all right.

8

Incarnation of Yama

Mansukhani began his examination of Devdutt. 'What's your sister's name?'

'Harini,' said Devdutt.

'Is it true that she and Krishnan had an intimate relationship?'

'Yes.'

'Is it true that this resulted in her having to consult a doctor?'

'No, not true.'

'Did you write a letter to Krishnan when you saw his wedding invitation?'

'Yes.'

'What did you write?'

'The letter's already been filed in court, Your Honour. I think this question is unnecessary,' said Ganesh.

'Yes. It is unnecessary,' agreed the magistrate.

Manuskhani continued: 'You wrote, "If that were to happen, I will kill you. Yes, I will kill you", and you had underlined those sentences. Do you admit that you wrote those sentences?'

'Yes.'

'You also wrote: "I have enough courage and dislike and reason to kill three men such as you". You wrote that too, didn't you?'

'Yes, I did.'

'Did you perhaps write it in jest?'

'No. My letter reflected my feelings at the time.'

'Are they the words of a man who respects human life?'

'They are the words of a man who respects human life, but who was angry when he wrote the letter.'

'Do you get angry often?'

'I am angry now.'

Ganesh glared at Devdutt. Mansukhani continued unrelentingly: 'You are capable of doing anything in a fit of anger, aren't you?'

'No.'

'How can a person's anger be reflected in a letter, but not in his actions?'

'Writing a letter is one thing. Doing as one threatens is another. They occur at different times.'

'Where were you at seven-thirty that night?'

'Seated before a piano.'

'Not in flat number 503, Tivoli Gardens?'

'No.'

'Perhaps you had murdered Krishnan in his flat and then …'

'You don't have to complete your question. My answer is, "No".'

'I say that you were not playing in the band that night.'

'You are wrong,' said Devdutt calmly.

'Your restaurant is on Mahatma Gandhi Road.'

'That's right.'

'It is possible for you to take a taxi from there to Pedder Road, isn't it?'

'Yes.'

'That's all,' said Mansukhani.

Ganesh resumed his questioning of Devdutt. 'What's the distance between Trincas and Tivoli Gardens?'

'About six kilometres.'

'Do you play continuously in the band? Or are you allowed breaks?'

'More or less continuously.'

'In case you have a break, what's the duration of the break?'

'Thirty seconds.'

'Do you have to be a part of the band for all songs?'

'Yes. Our band is a small combo. I have two roles to play—I sing and also play the piano.'

'Once you're through with a song, is it possible for you to make a dash to Tivoli Gardens and get back in time for the next song?'

'Only if I had a Boeing 707 at my disposal,' said Devdutt.

'That wraps up my defence,' said Ganesh.

When the hearing resumed, Ganesh analyzed the testimony of the prosecution witnesses. 'This is a fabricated case. A hurried fabrication. My question is why was Devdutt singled out? There must be others with a motive for the murder. Where are those others?

'Krishnan was a playboy. We should have a list of his friends. How many of them were women? Where were they on the night of the murder? We have no information about any of them.

'Inspector Madhavan has found that the shoeprints in Krishnan's room match those of Devdutt. So what does that prove? That Devdutt visited Krishnan's flat. We have never denied that. The inspector need not have wasted mercury chalk powder. We admit that Devdutt visited Krishnan's flat. He did go there. But when did he go there—that's the question. The prosecution argument is that the time of Devdutt's visit to the flat coincides with the time given in the post-mortem report as the time of Krishnan's death. Prosecution has produced three witnesses: taxi driver Mr. Charandas, Mr. Sheroor, and Mrs. Dastur. Charandas could be right about the time. It's possible that he dropped off a man at Tivoli Gardens at seven-thirty. But we cannot accept his statement that that passenger was Devdutt. That is a police concoction. Taxi drivers can't remember the faces of all their passengers. The next day at the police station, the police point to Devdutt and repeatedly ask Charandas, "Is this the man?" until he says it is. That's an old technique.

'The next witness—Sheroor. The time he gave, his reason for being on the fifth floor, etc. can't be accepted. They are just a pack of lies.

'Mrs. Dastur. She said she heard Devdutt and Krishnan argue. Her testimony doesn't mention the time of that argument. Prosecution didn't question her about this either. A very important thing about her statement is that she did not hear any music when the argument was going on. She only heard the argument. If Devdutt had strangled Krishnan to death, would she not have heard Krishnan's last throaty gasps for breath? Would the two men not have upset chairs and tables if they had fought with each other? And if so, would Mrs. Dastur not have heard the sounds of the scuffle?

'The inspector said the record player was running when he visited the flat. When the murder took place, a record must have been playing. It could have been a clever move on the part of the murderer to drown out sounds of any struggle. But Mrs. Dastur heard no music—only an argument. So what does this show? It shows that the murder and Devdutt's visit to the flat took place at different times.'

Ganesh sat down.

Mansukhani summed up the prosecution arguments and said Devdutt's alibi was weak. 'The defence lawyer wondered why no sounds of a struggle were heard. Devdutt is tall and well-built. Krishnan had no suspicion of Devdutt's intentions. In such a case, when the element of surprise was in favour of Devdutt, Krishnan would have been too shocked and too traumatized to shout when Devdutt slipped a rope around his neck and began to strangle him.' Mansukhani argued that the police had made out a strong case against Devdutt. He completed his arguments and sat down. He knew what the outcome would be.

Magistrate Purushottam Haridas looked at his watch. 'We will resume at three-forty-five,' he said.

'You were great, Ganesh,' said Harini.

'Wait. Let's see what the magistrate says.'

There was a slight tremor in Ganesh's fingers as he lit a cigarette.

Magistrate Purushottam Haridas took his seat at three-forty-five.

He took off his spectacles, wiped the lens and said, 'After hearing the arguments of both sides, and after examination of the prosecution witnesses and the defence witness, the conclusion is that there is no evidence to show that Devdutt committed this crime.'

'Hurray,' said Devdutt, and both the magistrate and Ganesh looked at him sternly. Harini was wiping tears from her eyes.

The magistrate continued, 'The prosecution case is weak. Hurried. Insufficient. There is no evidence to commit the case to sessions. Devdutt should be released.'

'Very weak prosecution,' muttered Mansukhani and left the court.

Harini, Devdutt and Ganesh had downed three cups of coffee.

'Ganesh, excellent. Terrific.'

'Easy. Save some adjectives for later use.'

'I want to say "thank you" a thousand times. Shall I begin now?'

'My visit to Krishnan's flat that night looking for Harini's letters, and your letter to Krishnan, is what led the police to hurriedly come up with their version. In their haste, they focused all their attention on misleading clues. Still, it was a close shave,' said Ganesh to Devdutt.

'Now that it's been proved that I am not the murderer, who did it?'

The waiter came with the bill.

'Why, it could be this man,' said Ganesh. 'That's the problem of the police department. Right now my interest lies elsewhere,' said Ganesh, giving Harini a meaningful look. 'Harini, will you come to my room and have a look at my pencil sketches?'

'Yes,' she said. That 'yes' was loaded with meaning.

'What will happen to this case now?' she asked.

'Why should you worry about it? The police will close the file after a few days. Or it may go to a higher official in the police department. He may investigate unexplored angles, if any, to the case.'

From Sunanda's diary

What would I do if I had two hundred thousand rupees? I wouldn't know how to spend it. I will print my brother's first novel. Will that cost ten thousand rupees? I'll not only have to print his novel, but also buy all the copies. No one can understand what he writes. He says, 'You are all so dense that it will take at least five hundred years for you to understand what I am saying.'

9

Ramanathan

Superintendent Viswanathan Ramanathan was mechanically pulling out the petals in the garland of roses. He was waiting for the vote of thanks. The speakers had come up with the most ingenious lies in their attempt to praise him. That was because he was due to retire in a fortnight. There was nothing sincere about their praise. A month later, the same people will say, 'Ramanathan? That old goose!'

The long-winded speeches gave him time to cast his mind back over his twenty-nine years of service in the Bombay Police Department. He had joined the service in the days of the British Raj, and had risen through the ranks steadily.

'I didn't take the IPS shortcut,' thought Ramanathan. Twenty-nine years! Twenty-nine years packed with varied incidents! Twenty-nine years! Years of turmoil and peace too. Pistols fired in the air, use of tear gas, toxicology, medical jurisprudence, long, tiring waits in Sessions Courts, that unforgettable suicide, the girl who jumped from the eighth floor into the middle of peak hour traffic, the drops of blood at the corner of her lips. Arrack, brewed illicitly in a hut, and transported in car tubes … Judges, the death sentences they had handed down, charging at mobs with batons, slippers hurled at the police … Twenty-nine years.

And now I am going to be free of all this.

'Ramanathan's uprightness, discipline …'

That is Bhaskaran. He is in an expansive mood because he's going to get a promotion. Hence all the superlatives about me. Bhaskaran is an entertaining rascal.

At the end of the farewell, just as he was about to get into his car, Ramanathan asked the deputy, 'What happened to the Pedder Road case? Why did the case not stand up to judicial scrutiny?'

'That was an arrest made in haste, sir. Dismissed at the preliminary stage itself,' said Bhaskaran.

'Who was in charge of investigation?'

'Madhavan. Inspector. I supervised the investigation.'

'Madhavan is an intelligent police officer.'

'He was a bit hasty.'

'Why don't you say "We were hasty"?'

Bhaskaran laughed.

Ramanathan continued. 'I know you were hasty. But why?'

'Sir, we had strong evidence against the suspect. We were sure we had done a good job. But the police case wasn't presented properly at the hearing.'

'I should have taken some interest in this case. I was preoccupied with the labour unrest in that factory. Anyway, I want all the papers pertaining to that case. I'll study them today. Ask Madhavan to come and meet me tomorrow. Right?'

'Right, sir. Good night.'
'Good night.'

—

While at the traffic signal, Ramanathan's thoughts turned to the Pedder Road murder. *I'm going to retire in fifteen days. And I'm going to leave behind an unsolved murder. Murder—a crime of emotion. The police won't see it as a significant crime. Still … I want to ease my conscience. I must have a look at the papers.*

The light turned to green. The car sped on.

Rohini was up reading when Ramanathan arrived.

'Dad, how was the party?'

'The usual. I was the hero. If those who spoke were to be believed, then there couldn't be anyone more saintly than yours truly. Beside me even Gandhi and Albert Schweitzer would seem wicked. The most blatant lies!'

'Dad, you are a cynic.'

'I'm a policeman. And I am familiar with lies. My dear girl. It's late. You must go to bed.'

'What about you?'

'I have to read some files.'

'About the Krishnan murder case?'

'How did you know?'

'This afternoon I read all the documents relating to that case.'

'Have you nothing better to do?'

'I was bored …'

Ramanathan thought of his dead wife.

'Dad, don't mistake me. But I think the police have been hasty and confused in this case.'

'Really?'

'Devdutt can't be the murderer. Someone else is the murderer.'

'Excellent, my dear daughter. Now tell me who the murderer is. I'll get you a Coke if you tell me who it is.'

'That's for you to find out.'

'I'm about to retire. I have to put my pension papers in order. I have to get you married. I have to earn more money. I'm afraid to go back to south India after having lived here for so many years. I don't want to be idle post retirement. So many things to worry about. And now this case has to be solved.'

'Do you have to solve this case?'

'I don't have to. But this is a challenging case, and I like challenges. I have fifteen days to go for retirement. So I have fifteen days to solve this murder.'

'Don't worry, Dad. You'll solve the mystery. I like the name Krishnan. No one called Krishnan should die. If someone has murdered a man called Krishnan, then the murderer must be found and punished.'

'No one should be murdered, period. But do you know how many people are being murdered now, this minute, as we are having this conversation?'

'No, I don't.'

'Neither do I. Okay. Go to bed. You have to get up early tomorrow morning—eight-thirty, right?'

She laughed and left the room. Ramanathan turned on

the table lamp and began to read about Krishnan. He took a sheet of paper, sharpened a pencil, and put down some points. Here are the points he wrote down. Read them to see if you can make out what he is trying to say:

Taxi driver?

Charandas is telling the truth.

Where did he come from? Mahatma Gandhi Road.

Go to Mahatma Gandhi Road. Look at the place.

Seven-thirty to eight-thirty in the evening.

What about Harini? Meet her.

Telephone numbers?

Diary?

Where did Krishnan live in the last three or four years?

So many errors.

Shoeprints. Nothing extraordinary about this.

Jazz records. Which of Krishnan's friends likes jazz?

What do I know about the X who committed the murder?

1. Strong man—hyoid bone broken. Or it could be that his hatred for Krishnan gave him extraordinary strength. Why? Three reasons, etc.
2. Definitely someone Krishnan knew. Whisky, record player, coffee.
3. Man—shoeprints? The man the taxi driver dropped off?
4. Pre-meditated.

Mister X. Here I come.

Sleepy ...

RAMANATHAN

Madhavan visited Ramanathan the next morning. Saluted Ramanathan. Sat on the sofa.

'I studied the case file yesterday night. You've missed out some very important points,' said Ramanathan.

'I don't think we missed out anything, sir.'

'Listen to what I have to say. You'll see what I mean. The FIR, investigation report—I read everything. That lawyer—what's his name?'

'Ganesh, sir. You mean the defence lawyer, don't you?'

'Yes, that's the man. He was able to point out all the lapses in the police investigation. As far as Devdutt is concerned, the time element is completely wrong. You should have known that right at the beginning.'

'Sir ... Shall I tell you why we suspected Devdutt?'

'No. I am not interested in lame excuses. I want to concentrate on what needs to be done. There are fifteen days to go for my retirement. I'm an old-fashioned policeman. I don't want to close this file with a question mark hanging over it. I'm going to find out who the murderer is. Definitely. My approach is different. An unhurried approach. An approach based on psychology. It's the method where, if two plus two doesn't add up to four, I ask why. Do you understand?'

'Yes, sir.'

'Right. I have made some notes. The taxi driver Charandas. You questioned him, didn't you?'

'Yes.'

'That night—the night of the murder. Did you find out if there were visitors to any of the other flats in the building?'

'I did, sir. No one had any visitors that night.'

'Why did you not bring that to the notice of the court? You should have. So we know that the man Charandas brought to the building that night was someone who came to meet Krishnan …'

'And that is why—'

'Please do not interrupt. The taxi driver came to the police station of his own accord, didn't he?'

'Yes.'

'Asking him to point to Devdutt as his passenger was a big mistake.'

'But our legal system requires incontrovertible proof, sir.'

'Don't talk to me about the legal system. Madhavan, your report is a good one. But there's something missing. Did Krishnan have a book with phone numbers? Phone numbers of people he knew. Did you find any such diary or notebook?'

'There was a diary. We checked every one of those numbers. I've even given a list of the numbers in my report.'

'How did you make enquires?'

'I met everyone on that list in person.'

'Did you clear everyone on Krishnan's list?'

'All, except one.'

'Which one is that?'

'There were eighteen numbers in the list. Seventeen out of the eighteen numbers turned out to be phone numbers of individuals. Krishnan's friends, girlfriends. Every one of them had an alibi, except Devdutt.'

'What is that eighteenth number which you didn't check out?'

'It's the phone number of a factory. It's in Kurla Industrial Area. I've mentioned that in my report. Phone number 551583.'

'Did you go there and make enquires?'

'I did. It's a factory. Run by a Gujarati. They make iron grilles. There was no connection between Krishnan and that factory. I thought Krishnan must have got the number wrong.'

'Wrong conclusion. That telephone number holds the secret.'

'How do you know?'

'That's my guess. Let's go.'

'Where?'

'To that factory. What's the name? ... D. G. Engineering Works.'

―

Kurla. Ramanathan stopped the jeep some distance away from the factory. He was not in his uniform. 'You stay here, Madhavan. I will go to the factory. You come there fifteen minutes later.'

'All right, sir.'

Cows, cycles, dabbawallahs, textile shops, the smell of sweat, conversations in Marathi ... Ramanathan walked past the textile shops, past the hardware shops, past the cinema theatre, past little workshops, and reached D. G. Engineering Works.

Ramanathan looked round. Noon. A man was working with a drilling machine. The shrill sound of the machine cutting through iron.

There were two old lathes. There was a picture of Lakshmi, the Goddess of wealth, on the wall, beside the registration certificate of the factory. A glass partition marked off the manager's room. He could be seen talking on the phone. A small factory.

Ramanathan knocked and entered.

'Good afternoon.'

The manager indicated a chair with a slight inclination of his head. Ramanathan sat down. The manager continued his conversation with a Desai about a business transaction. When the telephone conversation ended, the manager said, 'What can I do for you?'

'I want an iron grille made.'

'One?'

'Yes.'

'Sorry. We don't take small orders.'

'But I saw a welding machine.'

'That's for our routine jobs. There are other workshops that take small orders. A furlong from our factory …'

'Krishnan sent me here,' said Ramanathan, watching the manager carefully. 'Krishnan. G. N. Krishnan, Pedder Road. Tivoli Gardens.'

'I'm sorry. I don't know anyone called Krishnan.'

'Aren't you the manager?'

'Yes, I am.'

'Don't you know Krishnan?'

'No.'

'How many people are employed in your factory?'

'Ten. Are you from the police?'

'Yes.'

'Fifteen days ago, an inspector came here to enquire about this Krishnan. We told him we didn't know anyone called Krishnan. He talked to all the employees. There must be some mistake. I'm twenty-eight years old. The only Krishnan I know is Lord Krishna of the *Mahabharata*. We are a respectable organization. We pay all our taxes. We don't know this Krishnan. There's some confusion somewhere.'

'Your name?'

'Patel.'

'Mr. Patel. You know that lying to the police is an offence, don't you?'

'I don't know Krishnan.'

'Krishnan has been murdered.'

'May his soul rest in peace. What else can I say?'

From Sunanda's diary

I, the great!

Question: Why does Sunanda refuse to see Mr. Y?

Answer: Krishnan.

Question: Why is Sunanda very happy?

Answer: Krishnan.

10

Motive for the Murder

Madhavan walked towards Ramanathan. 'Sir, did you get any information?' he asked, although he knew the answer would be in the negative.

'No. But the manager doesn't seem to be lying. However, I have a hunch that the secret lies in that phone number. Did you talk to all the employees of that factory when you were there?'

'I did, sir. Most of them are Marathi-speaking. I don't think there is any connection between Krishnan and this factory.'

'But the telephone number of this factory is in Krishnan's diary. Madhavan, what had Krishnan written beside that number?'

'Only the letter "J".'

'Who or what is J?'

'Search me, sir.'

'That diary is an old one. The numbers in that diary must have been ones that Krishnan called often. It's possible that the number might have changed. Were any numbers in the diary scored out and new ones put in their place?'

'Yes.'

'If even one of the digits in the number had changed, Krishnan would have corrected it in his diary, wouldn't he?'

'So?'

'There's nothing wrong with the number. Arrange to keep a watch on this factory. Maybe they are engaged in something illegal.'

'Okay, sir.'

'I'm going home for lunch now. Come to my office this afternoon. We'll continue the hunt …'

'A hunt where we remain blindfolded, sir.'

'We won't be. Not for long. Don't worry.'

'Who is this Krishnan?' asked Ramanathan, when Madhavan met him in the afternoon.

'I've given details about Krishnan in the appendix to my report. Shall I read it out?' asked Inspector Madhavan.

'No. Just consult your notes and answer my questions. Right?'

I must count the number of times this man says 'right', thought Madhavan.

'Full name?'

'G. N. Krishnan.'

'He was from?'

'He was a Madrasi.'

'I don't like that word. There are many areas south of the Vindhyas. Everyone from the south isn't from Madras. Do you know the name of my village? Therazhundur. Try saying it. I'll give you five rupees if you pronounce it right.'

'I'll lose the bet, sir.'

'Where was Krishnan from?'

'Kerala. A place called Thiruvalla.'

'Educational qualifications?'

'Mechanical engineering. Petroleum technology. M. Tech from Kanpur IIT. He was working as a manager in a private company in Bombay.'

'Married?'

'No. But he was engaged to be married. This could have caused some resentment among his girlfriends.'

'How long had he been in Bombay?'

'Two years.'

'When did he pass out of IIT?'

'Five years ago.'

'Details about his previous employment?'

'He got his M. Tech degree in March, 1963. He was in Barauni for two years, and then in Delhi where he worked for the Indian Oil Corporation for six months. And then he took up this job in Bombay.'

'Any unaccounted-for period?'

'No. Kanpur. Barauni. Delhi. Bombay.'

'The murderer is in one of these four places.'

'Maybe.'

'Most probably Bombay.'

'How do you know?'

'That telephone number. What does it mean? J! A, B, C, D, E, F, G, H, I, J! All right. I'm going to meet that murderer in a fortnight.'

'Let's hope so.'

'What was Krishnan like in his private life?'

'In office, he was disciplined. In his private life …'

'Yes?'

'Women. Whisky. Parties. His neighbours gave us this information.'

'Did he have many girlfriends?'

'Many.'

'Can we say that a girl figures in this murder?'

'Definitely. The murderer stole nothing from Krishnan's flat.'

'Did you meet all of Krishnan's girlfriends?'

'I did. It was my duty to meet them, sir.'

'And did those meetings reveal anything?'

'Not much, sir. Krishnan gave them false assurances and had … you know what I mean, sir. Krishnan had lots of money at his disposal.'

'Did you have a look at his cheque book? Had he given anyone any large sums of money recently?'

'Yes, to Harini.'

'Let's leave Harini out of this discussion. It's been proved that she and her brother were not involved in this murder.'

'I'm still not convinced about that. I'm sure Devdutt is the murderer.'

'No. Not Devdutt. You'll see when I am through with this case. Let's come to the taxi driver Charandas. He brought a passenger to that building. That's certain, isn't it?'

'Yes, that's certain.'

'How can you be sure?'

'The next morning Charandas read about the murder in the newspaper and told us that he'd dropped off a tall man at the building the previous night.'

'A passenger he picked up from Mahatma Gandhi Road?'

'Yes.'

'Where on Mahatma Gandhi Road did he pick up this passenger?'

'Near Jehangir Art Gallery.'

'Let's go there. I might get some clarity if we visit the place.'

'I visited the place, sir.'

'You and I might view the same thing differently, Madhavan. Wait a minute. Let's not go now. We should be there at seven-thirty in the evening, the time when the taxi driver picked up his passenger.'

'What difference does it make?'

'I'll tell you later, Madhavan.'

―

Evening. The jeep was emerging from Hornby Road onto Mahatma Gandhi Road. Ramanathan told the driver to drive slowly. He looked around as the jeep moved slowly along Mahatma Gandhi Road. Shops. Cars. Cars that went past at a terrific speed. It seemed as if they were leaping like tongues of flame. Caucasian sailors walking on the pavement. Lazy men, hoping for a tip in dollars, following them, like the lamb that followed Mary.

The jeep went past Jehangir Art Gallery and went up

to the Gateway. Ramanathan asked the driver to turn back: Yacht Club Road, Taj Mahal Hotel … Ballard Pier. After some thought, Ramanathan said, 'Go back to the art gallery.'

He got down and said to Madhavan, 'Let's walk. Isn't this where Charandas picked up his passenger?'

'I brought him here, sir, and asked him to show me where exactly he picked up the man. He pointed to a place about a hundred and fifty feet from the signal. I'll show you the place, sir.'

They walked on in silence.

'This is the place, sir.'

'Let's stand here for awhile.'

'And do what?'

'Nothing. Let's just stand here.'

'All right,' said Madhavan with a sigh.

Ramanathan looked at his watch.

'Today is not a Sunday, is it?'

'No.'

'And the murder didn't take place on a Sunday, did it?'

'No.'

Ramanathan counted the taxis that went past them. After five minutes, he said, 'There is a taxi passing by roughly every twenty-five seconds.'

'Okay, sir.'

'So what do you infer from this?'

'Nothing.'

'The murderer must have come from some place nearby. He must have come from a place that can be reached from here in thirty seconds. If one walks fast, one can cover fifty feet in thirty seconds.'

He looked round.

'Look, Madhavan. What do you see there?'

'Where?'

'Look. There.'

'The Indian Airlines building.'

'Our murderer must have come from the Indian Airlines building.'

'I don't understand, sir. What makes you come to this conclusion?'

'Logic, my dear friend, logic! A man with an intention to kill boards a taxi here. A premeditated murder. There would have been a reason for every move of his before he committed the murder. If he had enjoyed a painting in the art gallery, or bought a shirt in a shop, or sipped some chilled coffee before the murder, then the man would be a psychopathic killer. He wouldn't be a normal person. But if we assume our friend is normal, then there must have been a reason for his boarding the taxi here. A journey would be a good reason, wouldn't it? Let's go to the Indian Airlines office.'

―

The girl at the enquiry desk in the Indian Airlines office welcomed them. They introduced themselves.

'Please talk to the traffic officer there.'

When he saw the men in police uniform, the traffic officer asked, 'How may I help you?'

'I want a list of passengers who travelled on the 16th, 17th, 18th, 19th and 20th of last month.'

'Which service?'

'Both Calcutta and Delhi.'

'There are four flights to Delhi every day.'

'I want all of them.'

'I'll get them ready for you tomorrow morning.'

They came out.

'Madhavan, until last night, I was groping in the dark. I still don't know who the murderer is. But I think the gap between me and the murderer is narrowing.'

The old man is crazy, thought Madhavan.

Letter dated 22nd December, from Mr. Kaul, deputy secretary—Home Ministry, Delhi

Dear Ramanathan,

Krishnamurthy spoke to me yesterday about you. There is no communication as yet from the Union Public Service Commission about the position in the Central Bureau of Investigation. I think it might be a good idea for you to come to Delhi. Come and meet me at the Central Secretariat, South Block, Room 128. Please have a look at the letter from the Bombay Police Department with regard to this.

11

Needed, Click

Ramanathan and Rohini were seated on the floor, surrounded by some papers. These were the passenger lists from Indian Airlines for the 16th to the 18th of the previous month. 'Can't make head nor tail of any of this, Dad,' said Rohini.

'You'll understand. Do what I asked you to do. Look at the lists. Find out which of the passengers who came here on the 16th, 17th or 18th from Delhi or Calcutta left the very next day. Just do that.'

'I don't think these lists are going to yield any useful information, Dad.'

'Why not? We have the name of every passenger who came in. The ticket numbers. We can tell if a passenger was vegetarian or non-vegetarian. Whether the passenger was a man, a woman or a child.'

'How very useful!' she said mockingly.

'Why? Isn't a person's name useful information?'

'Will a man who is planning a murder use his real name?'

'That's true. Why don't you just do what I asked you to? We might get some clues.'

'Just three more lists to go.'

Ramanathan read the letter from Kaul again. He wondered whether he should go to Delhi or not. 'I have to find another job. I can't be idle. I don't want to rust out. And there's Rohini to think of. I must get her married. I need money. Pension and gratuity won't be enough.'

'Ready,' she said.

'Okay. Who are the passengers?'

'I've got two lists: Delhi and Calcutta. Let's first have a look at the Delhi list—passengers who came from Delhi and left the next day.'

'How many in that list?'

'Nine.'

'How many men on the list?'

'Five.'

'Read the names.'

'Seshayyan K., Narasappa K. T., Shenoy S., Navalkar P. P. N., and Raman.'

'Initial of Raman?'

'No initial.'

'Date?'

'Came on the 18th. Left for Delhi on the 19th.'

'Get the manifest for those two days.'

She searched for the manifest, found it and gave it to her father.

'Let's see. Raman … this is our man!'

'How do you know?'

'Look. He brought no luggage with him. He arrived on

the morning of the murder, and left the next morning. But Raman is a very common name. It can't be his real name. As you said, a man who plans a murder so carefully would have travelled under an assumed name.'

'So, does that mean we have to look for a man in Delhi who goes under the assumed name Raman?'

'Wait, wait, Rohini. I'm constructing a building with a pack of cards. A building precariously balanced. Based on conjecture. The first guess is that the murderer was a man. Then there's the taxi driver's evidence. Other cards are the Mahatma Gandhi Road card, the IAC card, then the Delhi and Calcutta cards. Just a gentle blow and the whole pack will collapse. One card still remains the odd man out. That phone number. The phone number written against the English letter "J". The factory that that number belongs to. The connection between Raman and that phone number.'

'Dad, I think that number is wrong.'

'No, it's not. There is some connection between that factory in Kurla, the man Raman, and the murdered man Krishnan.'

'I think all three were involved in printing counterfeit currency. There must've been a misunderstanding between them … Why are you smiling, Dad?'

'Your imagination!'

'There has to be some connection.'

'A factory in Kurla with the phone number 551583. A passenger called Raman who arrives without any luggage and leaves the next day. An engineer called Krishnan, working for a petroleum company, who is murdered. What is the connection, my dear daughter?'

'And there is that mysterious letter "J", written beside that telephone number.'

'And then there's a police officer called Ramanathan, who is to retire shortly. And there's his daughter Rohini, who hates the word "marriage".'

'Dad, are you going to Delhi?'

'So you've read that letter?'

'Dad, why should you take up another job?'

'Okay. You tell me what I should do. Shall I go back to my village and become an agriculturist? Shall I get you married to a farmhand there?'

'Do you always have to keep worrying about my marriage?'

'This stupid society expects it.'

'The answer is "No".'

'I am going to go to Delhi. This case keeps nagging at the back of my mind. There is a "click" moment in every case. One never knows when or how one will hear the click. But once you do, everything will fall into place. All you see now is an outline. A shadowy outline. A face lies hidden somewhere in that shadow. Click! Light! Everything becomes clear. And then the case is solved.'

'Click,' said Rohini.

'No. No use. I must hear that click in my brain. In my experience a click moment has never failed.'

A week of watching the Kurla factory showed that there was nothing shady going on there.

NYLON ROPE

Madhavan sought permission to close the file. Ramanathan gave no definite answer to him. He was busy with the withdrawal from his Provident Fund account. He then reserved a ticket for himself to Delhi. He bought a new toothpaste tube. He had his old suit dry-cleaned. He prepared to leave for Delhi.

The Frontier Mail was passing through the desert areas of Rajasthan.

In the dining car, Ramanathan was spreading butter on his toast. He could hear the conversation of two men seated behind him. They were talking about their bets on a horse race.

'Two hundred thousand rupees, sir. I should have got it. But I lost.'

'Really?'

'Sir, do you believe in dreams?'

'Why do you ask?'

'I had a dream the night before the race. A little girl appeared in my dream, and wrote a number on a slate. "Uncle, see if this is right", she said to me.'

'What had she written on the slate?'

'A five-digit number—58216. I remember so vividly. When I woke up, I thought there must be some significance to the dream. I placed my bet on that number—58216—Mahalakshmi's Indian League Jackpot.'

'Did it win?'

'Win? Not one of the horses. Not five ... not eight ... not two ...'

'And?'

'But on the same day, the jackpot number in the Madras Race was 58216. Prize—two hundred thousand rupees.'

'What a shame!'

Ramanathan dropped his fork. He heard a 'click' in his brain very clearly.

From Sunanda's diary

The human body—how wonderful it is! I have massaged my body so many times during my oil bath. It has meant nothing to me. My brother has sometimes accidentally bumped into me. I've felt nothing on such occasions. But today, when Krishnan patted my cheek and pressed my arm, how different it was!

What are the colours I like? Blue, blue, blue. The sky is blue. The deep waters of the ocean are blue. The jamun fruit is blue. Poison-blue.

12

You've Come to the Wrong Place, Mister

I'm the king of fools! thought Ramanathan. *What an easy clue! And it took me so many days to get it! What a fool I was not to have realized that the telephone number was a Delhi number and not a Bombay one. And having that factory in Bombay watched—it was a complete waste of time. Ramanathan, you emperor among fools! That 'J' lived in Delhi. He was the Raman who'd travelled to Bombay. He came to Bombay and left in a hurry. His Delhi number was 551583. Delhi! Not Bombay.* Ramanathan gave the waiter a more generous tip than usual.

Delhi was cold. Ramanathan stepped out of the Frontier Mail and looked around for the person who was supposed to meet him at the station. His tension was palpable. The tension of a man who has drawn two Aces in a game of cards, and is about to pick his third card. Two days to go for his meeting with the official from the Home Ministry. Two days to find 'J' and talk to him … *Mister J! Here I come. Where's the man who was supposed to be at the station? Are my guesses right? Is my line of reasoning right? Am I going to meet the man whose image I have built up from my guesses and my reasoning? I'm anxious to know if I'm right. I've heard that there used to be artists capable of drawing a portrait with a big toe. That's what I've done—drawn a slender outline. The fact that there is a real person here who might correspond to that image fills me with pride. Is that surprising? That's the feeling that constitutes the essence of twenty-nine years of service in the police force.*

The man Ramanathan was expecting was not at the station. Maybe he hadn't received the telegram, thought Ramanathan.

'Kailash Colony,' he said to the taxi driver. The driver was glad—that was a long distance from the station. Therefore, more money.

Connaught Place, Parliament Street, Vijay Chowk. Roads that remind us of the history of Delhi. Vestiges of the white man's civic sense can be seen in the clean streets.

Safdar Jung's pale imitation of the Taj. Airport. Official residences of central government employees. Delhi—where the modern and the old alternate.

'I received your telegram just a while ago,' said Ramanathan's friend. 'Are you here in connection with a case?'

'No. I'm due to retire in three days. I'm expecting a deputation in the Home Ministry.'

'What kind of job?'

'In the Central Bureau of Investigation.'

'What kind of job in the Bureau?'

'Secret for now.'

'So secret that you can get the details from the Pakistan High Commission,' he laughed.

Ramanathan didn't laugh. He was too preoccupied with thoughts of 'J'.

The next morning, he had his bath, ate breakfast, picked up his friend's phone, and called directory enquiry.

'Good morning. I have a phone number. Can I have the address and the name in which it is registered?'

'Who is speaking?'

'My name is Ramanathan. Bombay Police Department. I need this information for an investigation.'

'Just a minute, please.'

The girl who answered the phone could be heard talking to someone. She came back on the line. 'Please call the telephone revenue department. They have the lists of names.'

'Can you give me their number?'

She gave him the number.

He dialled the number.

'Good morning. My name is Ramanathan. Bombay police. I have a phone number. I want the address and the name in which it is registered. The number is 551583.'

In a minute he got the name and address. R. Jayaraman; 15-A-17, Western Extension Area, Karol Bagh, New Delhi 5.

Evening. Noisy Ajmal Khan Road. A person from Salem selling sugarcane. A Tirunelveli man selling betel leaves. Namkeen Bandar—a sweet shop run by a refugee from Karachi. A Malayali's photo frame shop. A Multani's footwear shop. Ramanathan walked away from the noisy street. Two dogs in house number 15-A-51 watched him affectionately, and once he was past the house, they did their duty with a couple of feeble barks.

NYLON ROPE

Door number 50, 49, 48. Ramanathan's heart was beating fast. Not good for my health, he told himself. *What if at the end of all this I am wrong? I'll look silly*, he thought.

But Jayaraman begins with 'J'.

And the passenger on that flight was Raman.

15-A-17. Four flats at the junction where two roads met. A small veranda surrounded by plants. Steps leading up from the veranda. A flat to the right. One to the left. There was a radio in the flat. Full volume—destroying the peace and quiet of the street. He could see a tea shop on the road, and a shop called Novelty Book Store. Television aerials on the terraces of some houses, proudly proclaiming that these homes had televisions.

Two girls skipping, discussing an absent friend. 'Where does Jayaraman live?' Ramanathan asked.

'First floor. The house on your right,' they said, without stopping their game.

'Thank you,' he said, and went up the staircase. The door was closed. A yellow nameplate with 'Jayaraman. W.H.O.' written on it.

Ramanathan pressed the doorbell. He could hear it ringing inside the flat.

'Yes,' said a voice from inside.

A male voice.

Ramanathan could hear the sound of shoes as someone walked towards the door. The sound of a latch turning. The door opened.

He was tall. He must have arrived about five minutes ago.

He was still formally dressed, and had a half-torn letter in his hand. He must have been in the middle of tearing it up when Ramanathan pressed the doorbell.

'What do you want?' he asked. Pleasant voice.

'Mr. Jayaraman?'

'Yes.'

'You don't know me. But I know your parents. I want to talk to you.'

'What about?'

'May I come in? Can we sit down and talk?'

'Okay.'

He pointed to the sofa. Ramanathan sat down. Ramanathan was looking at the picture opposite him, at the cupboard overflowing with books, at the radio that was on.

'You said you knew my parents. How?'

Ramanathan thought of what he should say. Jayaraman repeated the question.

'Bournvita. Bournvita. Bourn-vi-ta,' sang the radio. The jingle ended with a *ding ding di ding*.

'Will you switch off the radio, please? We are going to talk about something serious.'

'Go ahead,' he said, without switching off the radio.

'Mr. Jayaraman. Do you know G. N. Krishnan of Bombay?'

He switched off the radio.

Was he shocked? Hard to tell. Had a wary look crept into his eyes? Was the hand holding the letter shaking? And if it was, could it be because of the cold? Or was it because he was afraid?

'G. N.?'

'Krishnan. Flat number 503, Pedder Road, Bombay.'

'No. Why?'

'I think you know him.'

'What is this? Who are you?' Yes, his hands were definitely trembling. He was seated on the sofa and he was shaking his legs. A sign of his nervousness? He was trying hard to look calm.

'I'm from the police. Bombay.'

'So?'

'On the 18th of last month, Krishnan—'

'But I don't know anyone called Krishnan.'

'You are lying.'

'Inspector.'

'I'm not an inspector. I'm a superintendent.'

'I don't know anything about your police hierarchy. I don't know why you are in Delhi. But I do know that the way you've barged into my flat and your aggressive manner against me are violations of my fundamental right to liberty and personal freedom. Your approach is wrong.'

'You killed Krishnan.'

'What do you mean? You are crossing all limits. I can't make head or tail of what you are saying. I don't have the time to listen to your absurd accusations. Please go away.'

Ramanathan clapped his hands. 'You speak very nicely, Mr. Jayaraman. On the day of the murder you travelled to Bombay by flight under the name of Raman.'

'If you keep on and on—'

'In the evening, you went to the Indian Airlines office, confirmed your return ticket, took a taxi and went to Pedder Road.'

He was silent now.

'You went to Pedder Road, met Krishnan in his flat, and killed him. Even while a record was playing on his record player. You used a rope to strangle him, broke his hyoid bone, and killed him. You, you, you murdered him. Jayaraman. You killed Krishnan.'

'This is the limit,' said Jayaraman.

'You killed Krishnan and returned to Delhi the next day.'

'Get out before something untoward happens. Get out, you idiot.'

Ramanathan gripped his shirt. 'Nobody calls me an idiot, young man,' he said. But Ramanathan began to have doubts. Had he made a mistake? His stringing together of the evidence—was it wrong? What a risk! He'd come into the man's house and accused him! What if he were wrong?

'Inspector. (He kept saying inspector, again and again.) I'm going to count up to five, and before I finish, you must be out of my flat. Otherwise, I'll have to deal with you differently. (He had noticed Ramanathan's hesitation.) You can see how well-built I am. Let go of my shirt.'

Ramanathan let go of Jayaraman's shirt. For half a minute he wondered if he had indeed made a mistake. Had there been any slip-ups in the gathering of evidence? Was this the wrong place? Did this man really not know Krishnan? What should he do now?

NYLON ROPE

'I'll be back again,' said Ramanathan.

'Inspector, your sunglasses,' said Jayaraman, and threw Ramanathan's glasses at him saying, 'Catch.' Ramanathan caught them.

'The next time, make sure you have all your facts right. Don't try to buy a sweet in a shop that sells stationery.'

'I will be back. Definitely,' said Ramanathan. Jayaraman banged the door shut. Ramanathan looked up. The windows were closed too. He crossed the road and went into the tea shop. He sat on a bench behind a shelf stacked with buns. He couldn't see Jayaraman's flat from there but he could see the common entrance to the building. He ordered a tea and watched the common entrance.

He sipped his tea for ten minutes and ordered another. He didn't finish his second cup. He paid for both the cups and got up in a hurry. Reason—a taxi stood before the building on the opposite side and there was Jayaraman with a suitcase in his hand, about to get into the taxi.

'Just a minute, young man. You can't run away,' said Ramanathan, and gripped Jayaraman's arm. 'There are five policemen waiting nearby, and they will come to my aid. Do you want to kick up a fuss in public? You've left behind your fingerprints in Krishnan's flat. And now there are your fingerprints on my sunglasses. Give up the hopeless struggle.'

13
Sunanda's Diary

'What should I do now?' asked Jayaraman. 'Raise my arms above my head?'

'No need to. Pay the taxi and come upstairs with me. We need to talk,' said Ramanathan.

Jayaraman spoke to the taxi driver in Hindi, paid him off, and went up to his flat, with Ramanathan following him.

'Where should I begin?'

The two men were seated on the sofa in Jayaraman's flat.

'Switch on the heater first. It's very cold … That's better. Tell me, Jayaraman. Why did you kill Krishnan?'

Jayaraman had recovered his composure. He looked at his nails. Looked up at Ramanathan. 'Reason … Just a minute. Why should I tell you all this? I must consult my lawyer first. You can't prove anything against me. The legal system will defeat you. No. I will not say anything.'

'Jayaraman. Whatever you tell me now is off the record. I have no paper or pencil with me. No tape recorder. I've taken a lot of trouble to collect information and make sense of it, and then I've come here. You can talk to me without any inhibitions. If someone were to question you later, you can always say that you said nothing to me. I just want to know the truth. I'm not interested in the police case. Our conversation will be like a discussion between two chess players, the loser and the winner analyzing their moves after the match. Now tell me. Why did you murder Krishnan?'

'Sunanda,' said Jayaraman.

'Who is Sunanda?'

'A girl.'

'Of course.'

'Wait,' said Jayaraman, and went up to the cupboard. He opened it, pulled out a box. He took out a diary. 'Read this. This is Sunanda's diary. You need to understand the background to that murder, and this diary will tell you a lot.'

Ramanathan flipped through the pages of the diary. On the very first page were the lines: *Whoever reads my diary without my permission will hang upside down in hell for a thousand years.*

Ramanathan looked up.

'She's not alive to give you permission. Read it. It'll take you at least half an hour. I'm not going to run away. There's only one way to enter this flat. I'll make some coffee for us. Okay?'

'Okay,' Ramanathan said.

He turned the pages of the diary. A diary that had no dates. (Excerpts from this diary have already been carried in this story.)

The letters slanted to the right. Bold letters, some of them written with a flourish, with unnecessary ornamentation. On some pages a signature which varied from just Sunanda to R. Sunanda. A whole page which had the sentence, *Vatsala is a fool.*

Sunanda.

Ramanathan began to read from her diary.

Just finished Daphne du Maurier's book. There is nothing to equal Rebecca.

Sunanda, you are wicked. You have become very bold. You are no longer afraid. You should never have agreed to what happened today. What happened today in the darkness of the staircase? No, don't write about it.'

The funny thing is that my brother, who is on an official tour, has asked Krishnan to keep an eye on me. You silly fool! My dear brother!

*

Yes!
Yes!
Yes!

*

Dear God, thanks a lot. For creating me. Thanks because I am eighteen. Thanks for making me lonely, for sending a handsome rogue called Krishnan into my life. For making me experience the force of his masculinity. For making me forget myself in a fire of desire for three nights. For the aches, for the tears, for the smiles, for making me hear the beating of my heart, for my uncontrollable desires—thank you, God. Did I do something wrong? I don't know. God, if what I did was wrong, please, please, forgive me. If what I did was wrong, would it have given me so much pleasure, so much joy? Was it joy, or was it sorrow? Why did the tears flow from my eyes?

Why did it happen? Because of my loneliness? When did I actually start yielding? Was it when I saw him standing at the door clutching jazz records? Was it when he began playing a record and my heart began to beat faster, keeping pace with the music? Was it when he switched off all the lights, one after another? Was it when he whispered those words in my ears?

When?

Krishnan's advice.

'Try everything once!'

'Right and wrong—these are manmade boundaries. There is no need for us to be bound by these manmade rules. It's enough if we keep to the rules God has laid down. Don't hurt others.'

(As if he is Buddha).

'We are not just machines that breathe.'

'Why do you think a person has a body? For experiments such as these.'

(No, no, no—that was me.)

'Your loneliness and mine needed relief. That is why this happened.'

'Krishna, apart from me, have you, have you …'

'Never. Do you think I am a playboy like Lord Krishna? You're the only one … I introduced you to a new experience. A new fire.'

Fire indeed it was!

A fire whose touch meant pleasure.

La la la! I'm mad!

*

I've heard that song 'Fever' at least a dozen times today. How true the last line is– 'What a lovely way to burn!'

*

I'm writing again after so many days. Why did I not write for so long? Was it my fear about …?

Two things worry me.

One—Krishnan has left without taking leave of me. What happened to all his promises? My brother said: 'Stupid rascal! He left without telling me where he was going. He settled all his bills. But he didn't tell me he was going.'

And he didn't tell me either.

I can't tell anyone. I cry when I am alone. My brother doesn't know why I am listless.

I've decided to tell him. I mustn't be afraid. What's the use of being afraid? How do I tell him? Should I say to him, 'I've done something wrong?' Should I say it in English or Tamil? It sounds a bit more polished in English.

I shed no tears as I write now. Why? Had I expected this would happen? Did I, perhaps, want this to happen? Do I expect Krishnan to come back? There are no letters from him. Does he know about this? But how could he know? How will I tell my brother? What will he do? Will he slap me? Will he break a glass tumbler? I want to tell him that my loneliness is the reason for what happened. I want to say it a hundred times. You paid no attention to me, but played bridge with your friends. Those long tours you went on. All that nonsense you kept speaking was beyond me. Those books in your library—I can't understand any of them. The Tchaikovsky symphonies you like. My loneliness. The life I've lived without a mother, without a father. With no solace, no comfort, a life surrounded by arrogant males.

How am I going to tell him?

*

I told him. He slapped me. 'Leave me alone. Don't say anything more,' he said.

I sat in the darkness of my room, sobbing. Half an hour later, he called out to me. He ran his hand through my hair comfortingly. He asked me if I was sure it was Krishnan. I nodded. He abused Krishnan in words I'd never heard before. He then said, 'Sunanda. You are only eighteen. Even assuming we search for Krishnan and find him and compel him to regularize things, you will be the one to suffer. How many months have you missed?'

I told him.

'I'll deal with Krishnan later. Now you are more important. You need to be freed from this burden. This is not the way to begin your life. Change your clothes. We are going out,' he said.

I only vaguely understood what he was suggesting. The place he took me to was neat. 'Please wait. Doctor inside,' said a board on the wall. There was a framed certificate that attested to the training the doctor had had in Germany. Medical books arranged neatly in a shelf. The doctor was about forty-five years old. My brother haltingly told him what had happened. The doctor kept saying, 'I understand.'

Then, to me, he said, 'You mustn't be afraid. I'm not going to hurt you. I'm like your father.' He took me into a room. He asked me for some dates. He examined me.

Came out and told my brother something. I couldn't hear all of it, for he spoke in a low voice.

'She's too young. We'll have it on Monday. Come at seven o'clock. She mustn't eat anything. I'll prescribe a tablet. She has to take that the previous night. We'll give her anaesthesia and she'll be unconscious for just about half an hour. I don't accept cheques. I want to be paid in cash. Remember seven o'clock, Monday.'

I am afraid.
I am afraid.
I am afraid.

Ramanathan finished reading the diary. Jayaraman, who had been waiting for Ramanathan to finish, said, 'Three days after that operation, she died.'

14

Edifice of Cards

'What?'

'Yes! Three days! She fell victim to the doctor's greed. Rusty knife. Sepsis. Internal haemorrhage! I didn't know this at first …'

'Wait a minute … The J mentioned in the diary …'

'That's me. I knew Sunanda since the time she was a child. I also knew her brother—Narayanan. That stupid guy didn't take anyone into confidence … he didn't know whom to consult … he decided to take her to that doctor. He thought he was doing her some good, and he took her there … I didn't know any of this at first. He was leaving for the hospital when I met him at his house. I asked him where Sunanda was. Hospital, he said. I asked him what was wrong with her. Abdominal pain, he said, after some hesitation. He looked nervous.'

'The surgeon botched up everything. She was in hospital for three days, in a semi-conscious state, drifting into consciousness every now and then. We were frantic those three days. We tried desperately to save her. The doctors we called in chided Narayanan. Their words, the cigarettes we smoked, the taxis we took to and from the hospital, they are all etched in my memory.

'I will never forget that Wednesday, sir. I remember the purohit arriving on his cycle. I remember the funeral rites. A few distant relatives and lots of friends turned up for the funeral. Their questioning glances and the way Narayanan walked around like a zombie ...

'Sunanda, my dear Sunanda, the girl I was in love with, was dead. Her body was consigned to the flames. She was burnt down to ashes. The day after the cremation, Narayanan was asked to pick up a bone from the ashes as part of the religious rites. That was the day on which Narayanan broke down. He cut his jugular vein with a blade. He bled to death.'

Ramanathan shuddered.

'Three nights of Krishnan's lust! And in just three days, two deaths. A brother and sister reduced to ashes by a man's lust. Tell me, Mr. Ramanathan. Should he not be punished? Krishnan—you just read how Sunanda melted for him. Do you know what he said about Sunanda? "She was good in bed." Rascal! Moneyed rogue.

'He was about five feet six inches tall. Deep-set eyes. A face like a child's. A slightly feminine face. A face that seemed to suggest a man who ached for love and comfort. The sort of face that evokes the motherly instinct of women. The sort of face that attracts women. It's a matter of psychology. A woman has a maternal feeling towards a man before her sexual desire takes over, before she even becomes romantically attached to him. He had a deep voice. An attractive voice. He lived in Delhi for only six months. He used to play bridge with us. He saw Sunanda. His interest moved from bridge to Sunanda. She changed too. No, she was made to change. He made her change. His approach becomes clear from the accounts in her diary. He took advantage of her loneliness. The beginning of her end started with jazz music playing in the background. He played the game very cleverly. No one, not even Sunanda's brother, suspected his intentions. Krishnan had just one aim—that girl's body! He was the sort of rogue who soon tires of a woman's body.

'Sir, what should one do with a person who is responsible for the death of a brother and sister? Should we file a legal case against him? What kind of case should be filed against him? Can we accuse him of rape? Superintendent, sir, I too have read the Indian Penal Code. It's not easy to prove a man's guilt. The law makes it difficult to prove rape. So many things to be done. A certificate to prove Sunanda's age. And having to establish in the cold, impersonal atmosphere of a court that the rascal was responsible for the death of a young girl. Is that easy? And if we do manage to prove it, what punishment will he be given? Six months in prison? A year, at the most? Is that enough? Tell me, is that enough?

'I read Sunanda's diary only after her death, and her brother's. Narayanan left a note for me before his death. It said, "Sunanda's diary is in the cupboard. Read it to understand what happened." Narayanan was an innocent man. A man who didn't know how to deal with the problem, a man who couldn't forgive himself when he knew he had messed things up, a man who blamed himself for his sister's death. A man who lost the will to live.

'When I finished reading the diary, I decided that I would punish Krishnan! You can't call it revenge. Who was Sunanda? Who was I to take revenge? But anyone who knew them and who knew of the reason for their tragic end would have thought it his duty to eliminate Krishnan. I gladly assumed that duty. I began to look for him. Finding him and killing him became my magnificent obsession. Krishnan was alive. A man who didn't deserve to be alive, was alive.

'My enquiry was more thorough than a police enquiry. I visited the Indian Oil Corporation, where he had been employed. He had not left a forwarding address with them. I met more than forty friends of his. No one knew where he had gone. But I kept trying. I didn't give up.

'One day, quite accidentally, I got to know where he was. I chanced upon the in-house magazine of a petroleum company. I was in my friend's house to watch television, and that's where I found this magazine. I saw Krishnan's photograph in the magazine, and the caption said that G. N. Krishnan had been appointed to a senior managerial post in the company.

'Thereafter my job of finding him was easy. I wrote to a friend in Bombay and asked him if Krishnan's phone number was listed in the telephone directory. He gave me Krishnan's phone number and address from the directory.

'I could hardly contain myself. I flew to Bombay. I confirmed my return ticket for the next day. I visited him in his flat. I strangled him with a nylon rope while jazz music played in the background. I saw his legs thrash about when he was in the throes of death. I felt a deep sense of satisfaction. When my fury began to abate, I felt like laughing out loud.

'I returned to Delhi the next day.

'I took precautions to ensure I wouldn't be found out. And then ... Forgetting what I had done was easy. I didn't read the Bombay edition of any newspaper. I wasn't agitated. I didn't pace up and down smoking a cigarette. I was not afraid. And believe it or not, I went to work the next day! I went to my office in the afternoon. The only emotion I had was a sense of satisfaction. A deep sense of satisfaction.

'I had almost expected your visit. I told myself, "If the police are clever enough to find me, then let them come to me." No one saw me enter or leave Krishnan's flat. No one knew that I knew Krishnan. By the way, how did you find out?'

'He had your telephone number.'

'Oh, yes. Smart work, sir. What was I saying? Oh, yes. I told myself, "Let the police come here. What can they do? They will arrest me. I will give my explanation. Or I will find a good lawyer who will demolish the case and get me out. Even assuming I don't escape, what punishment will the court hand down? Hanging? Or a fifteen-year sentence in prison?" I wasn't the least bothered either way. I am unmarried. My sister is married and lives in Kuwait. My parents are no more. No one to worry about me ... I did something that made me happy. I was prepared to lose a thousand days of my life for the sense of satisfaction I had. What are you going to do now? Arrest me? Oh dear, the coffee has turned cold.'

Ramanathan was silent for awhile. He then said: 'As far as you are concerned, you have punished Krishnan. This is an unusual case. As you rightly said, he would not have been punished by the law. The punishment you gave him was what he deserved. You were prosecutor, judge and executioner, all rolled into one. Your act called for bravery but wasn't it wrong for you to have taken the law into your hands? But still ...'

Ramanathan looked at his watch.

'I think this case has come to a conclusion. I feel like a lepidopterist who chases after a special butterfly, a rare butterfly, and manages to catch it. But to punish you in this case would be an anticlimax,' said Ramanathan.

'Moreover, today I am no longer a police officer. I have retired. My conscience will be clear even if I don't arrest you ...

'Your case is an edifice I built of cards, a pyramid I built right up to the top. Now I can blow down this edifice I built.

'Justice has been done outside the provisions of the Indian Penal Code. I am happy about that. As far as I am concerned, I don't know you ... Good night!'

Ramanathan left the flat, walked quickly down the steps, and went out into the cold wintry night.

Made in the USA
Monee, IL
03 May 2026